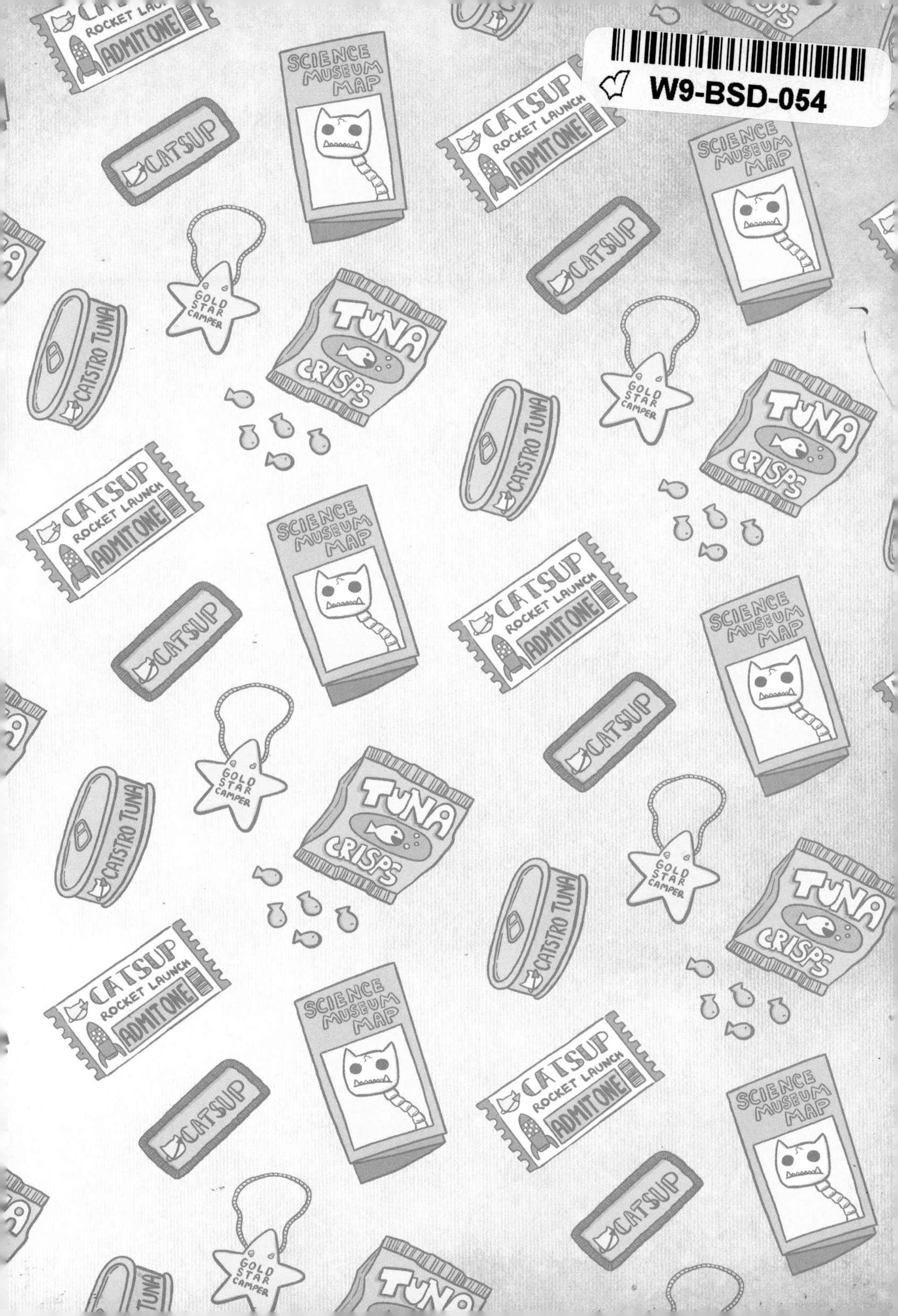
CATSUP
ROCKET LAUNCH
ADMIT ONE
SCIENCE MUSEUM MAP
CATSUP
GOLD STAR CAMPER
CATSTRO TUNA
TUNA CRISPS

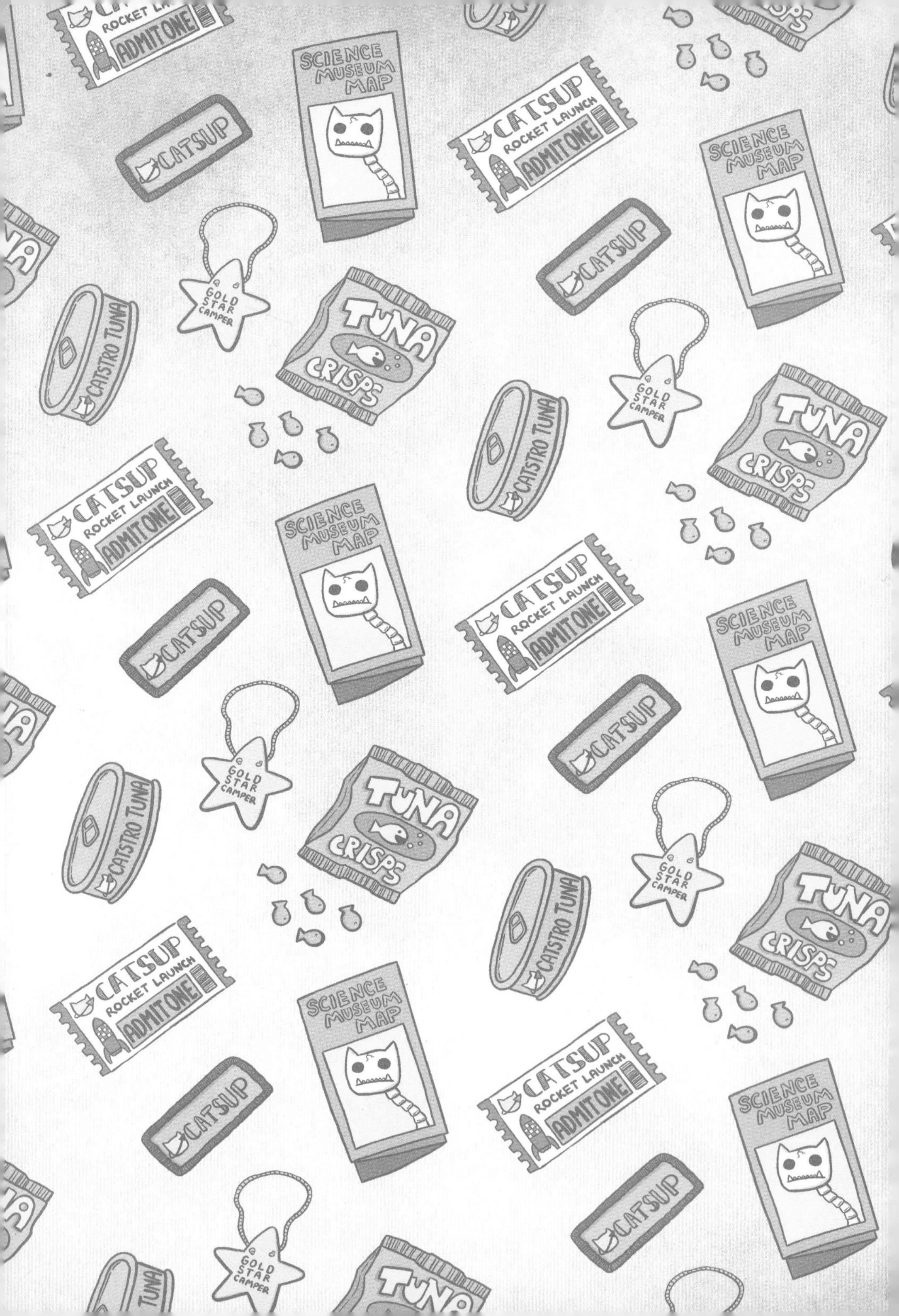
CATSUP
ROCKET LAUNCH
ADMIT ONE
SCIENCE MUSEUM MAP
CATSUP
GOLD STAR CAMPER
CATSTRO TUNA
TUNA CRISPS

A CATSTRONAUTS KITTEN ADVENTURE

WAFFLES AND PANCAKE

PLANETARY-YUM

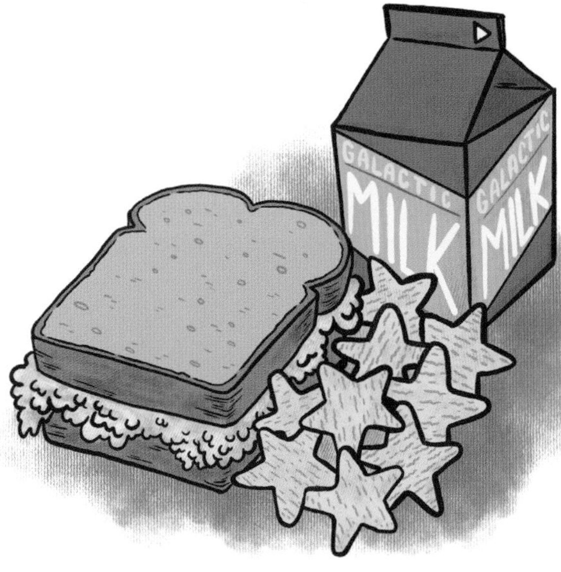
GALACTIC MILK
GALACTIC MILK

Noelle

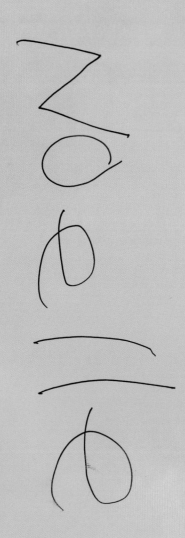

A CATSTRONAUTS KITTEN ADVENTURE

WAFFLES AND PANCAKE

PLANETARY-YUM

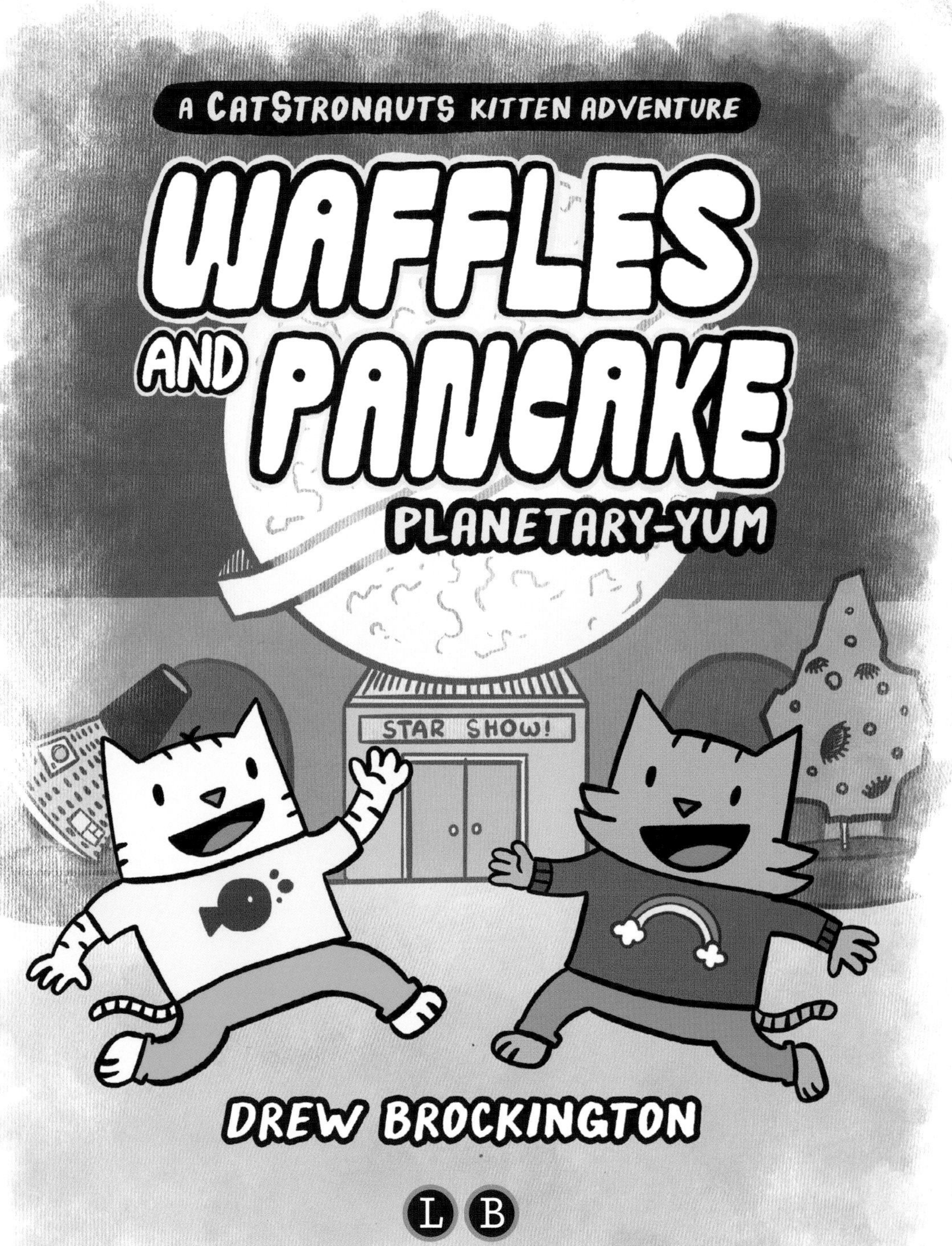
STAR SHOW!

DREW BROCKINGTON

LB
Little, Brown and Company
New York • Boston

About This Book

This book was edited by Rachel Poloski and designed by Ching N. Chan. The production was supervised by Bernadette Flinn, and the production editor was Jake Regier. The text was set in Colby, and the display type was created by Drew Brockington.

Little, Brown and Company
Hachette Book Group
1290 Avenue of the Americas, New York, NY 10104
Visit us at LBYR.com

First Edition: September 2021

Little, Brown and Company is a division of Hachette Book Group, Inc.
The Little, Brown name and logo are trademarks of Hachette Book Group, Inc.

The publisher is not responsible for websites (or their content) that are not owned by the publisher.

Library of Congress Cataloging-in-Publication Data

Names: Brockington, Drew, author, artist.

Title: Planetary-yum / by Drew Brockington.

Description: First edition. | New York : Little, Brown and Company, 2021. | Series: Waffles and Pancake | Audience: Ages 6–9. | Summary: Future CatStronaut Waffles and his younger sister, Pancake, are kittens who enjoy visiting the science museum with Dad-Cat.

Identifiers: LCCN 2020039912 | ISBN 9780316500425 (paper over board) | ISBN 9780316500418 (ebook) | ISBN 9780316500388 (ebook other)

Subjects: LCSH: Graphic novels. | CYAC: Graphic novels. | Cats—Fiction. | Science museums—Fiction. | Museums—Fiction. | Brothers and sisters—Fiction.

Classification: LCC PZ7.7.B76 Pl 2021 | DDC 741.5/973—dc23

LC record available at https://lccn.loc.gov/2020039912

ISBNs: 978-0-316-50042-5 (paper over board), 978-0-316-50039-5 (ebook), 978-0-316-50040-1 (ebook), 978-0-316-50041-8 (ebook)

PRINTED IN CHINA

APS

10 9 8 7 6 5 4 3

FOR ALANNA

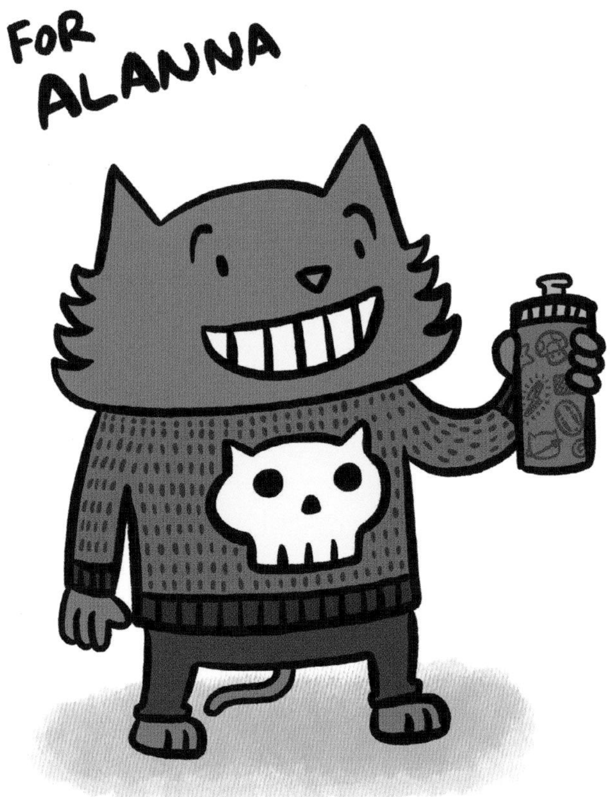

CHAPTER 1

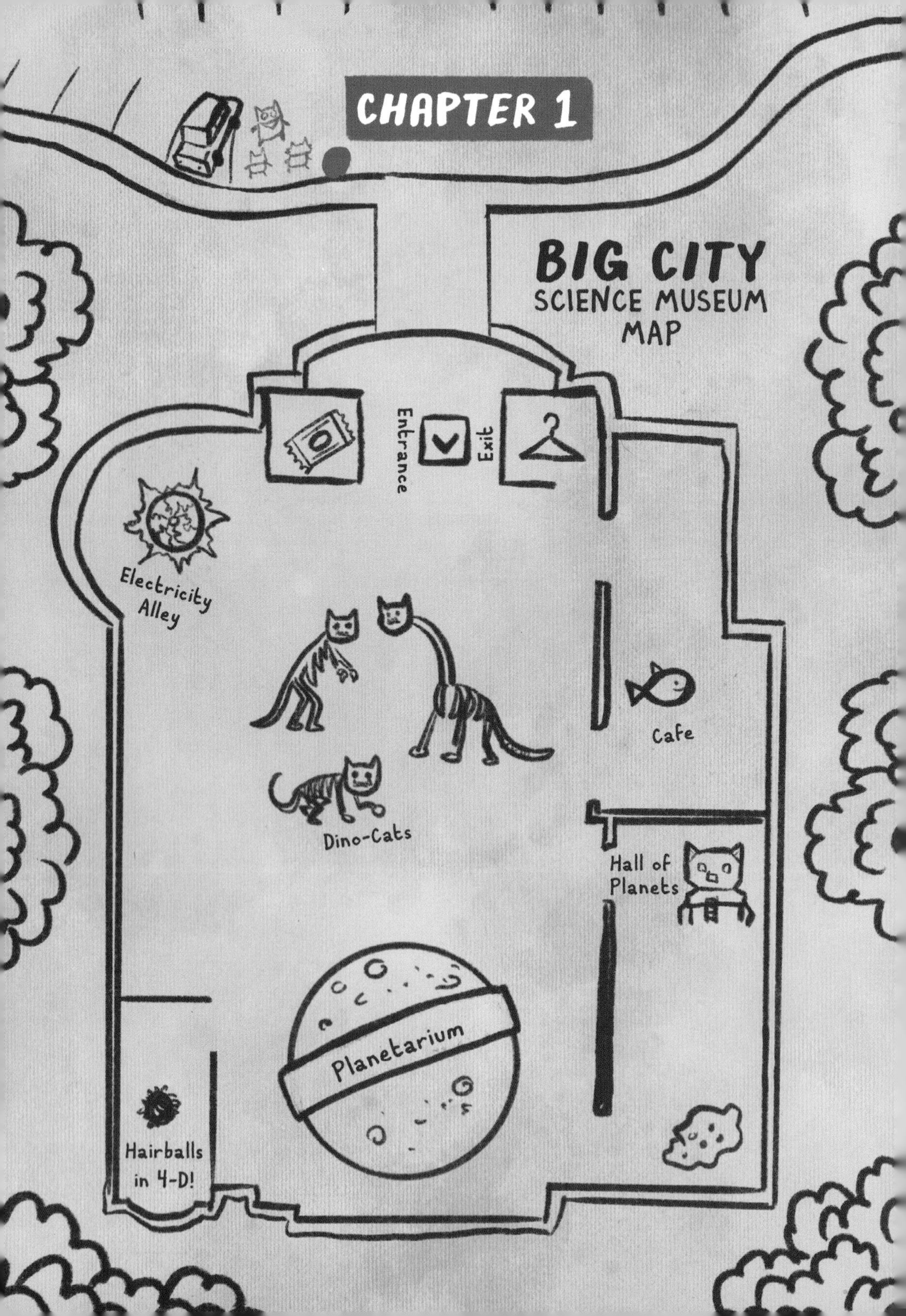

BIG CITY
SCIENCE MUSEUM
MAP
Entrance
Exit
Electricity Alley
Dino-Cats
Cafe
Hall of Planets
Planetarium
Hairballs in 4-D!

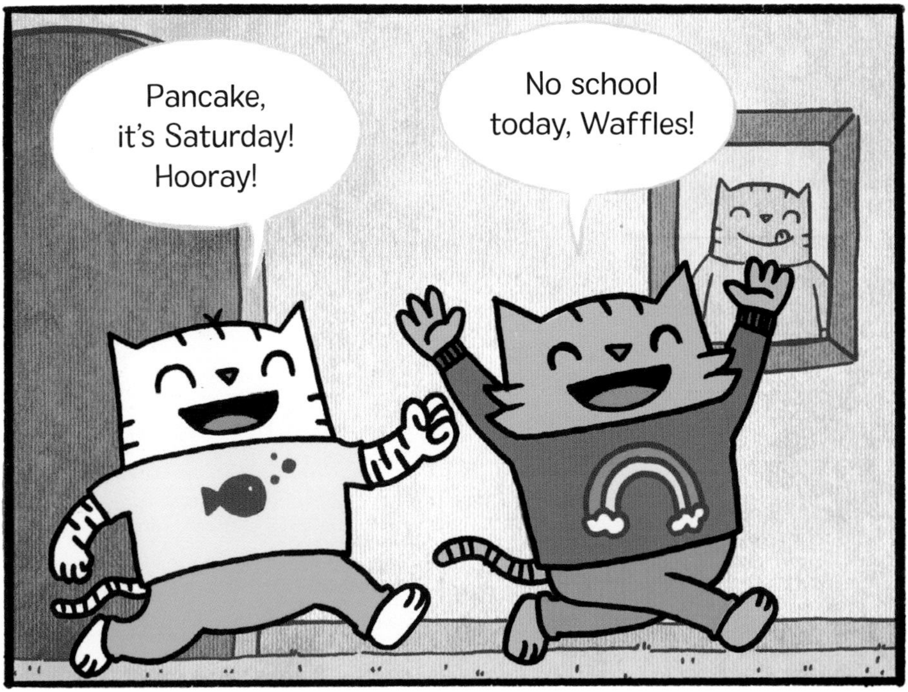
Pancake, it's Saturday! Hooray!
No school today, Waffles!

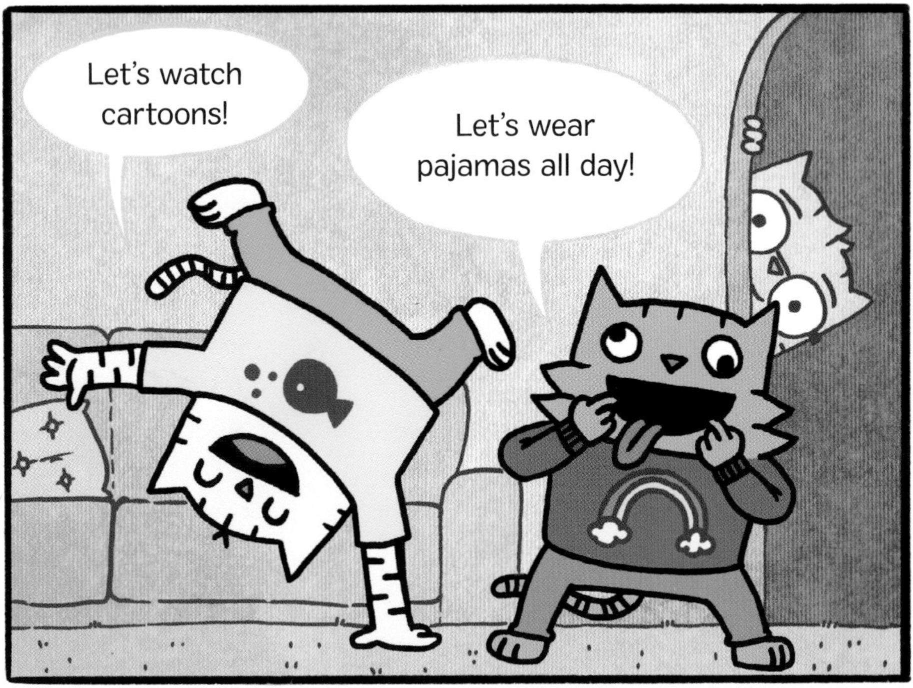
Let's watch cartoons!
Let's wear pajamas all day!

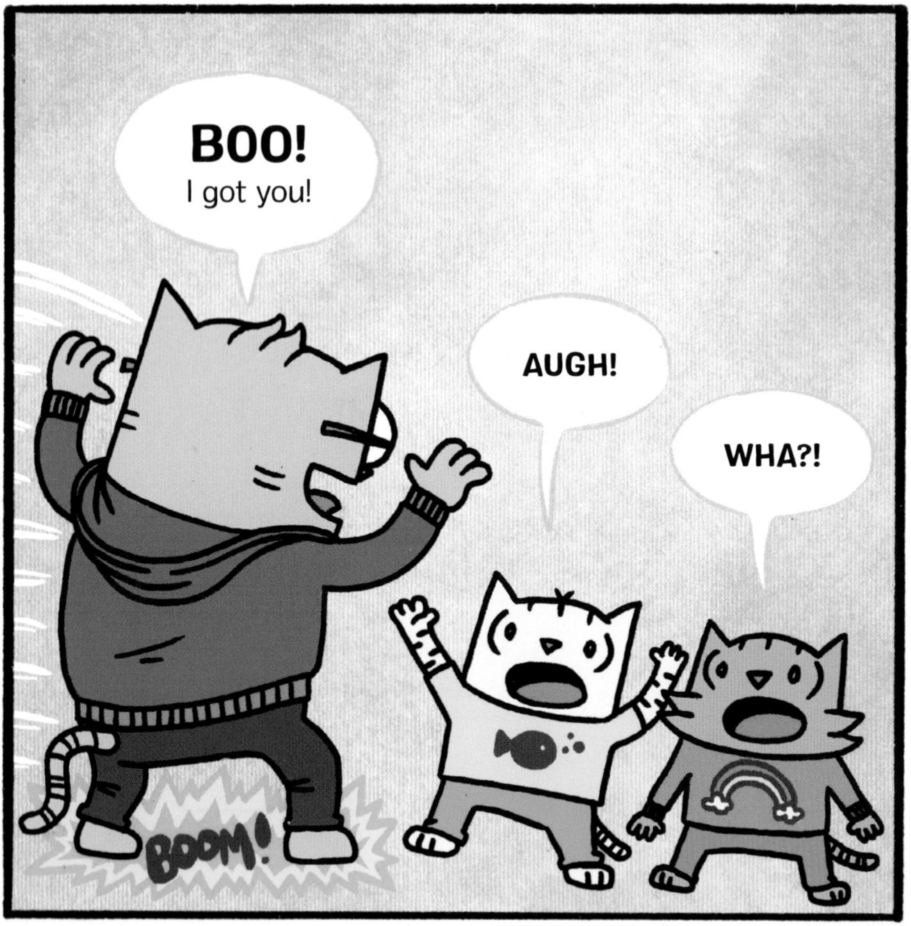
BOO!
I got you!
AUGH!
WHA?!
BOOM!

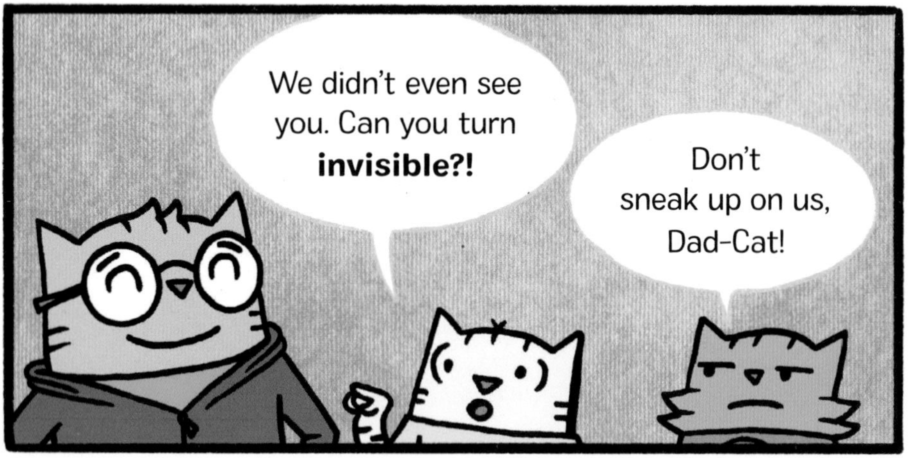
We didn't even see you. Can you turn **invisible?!**
Don't sneak up on us, Dad-Cat!

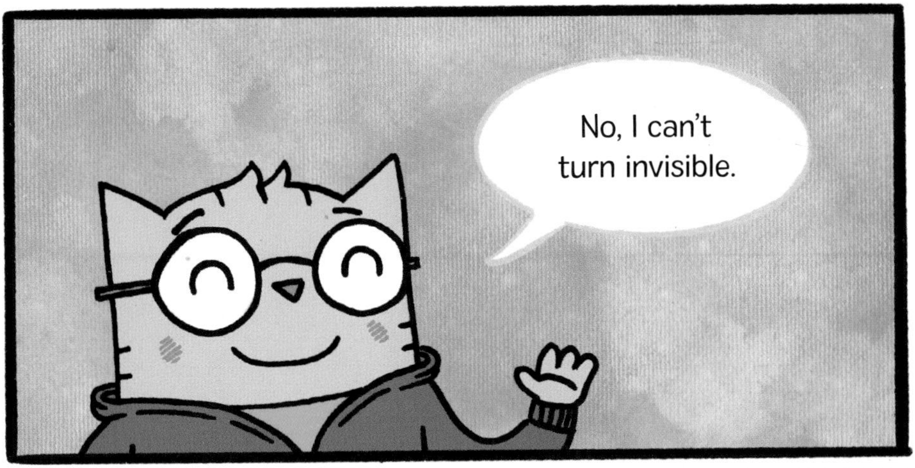
No, I can't turn invisible.

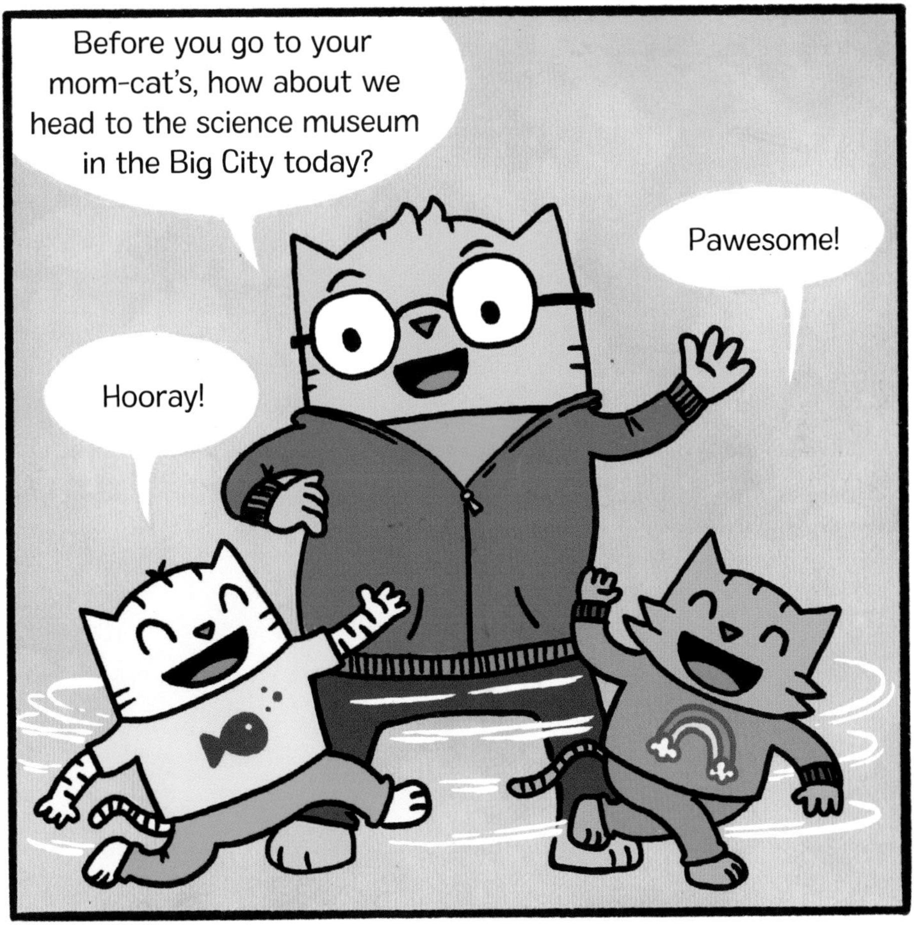
Before you go to your mom-cat's, how about we head to the science museum in the Big City today?
Pawesome!
Hooray!

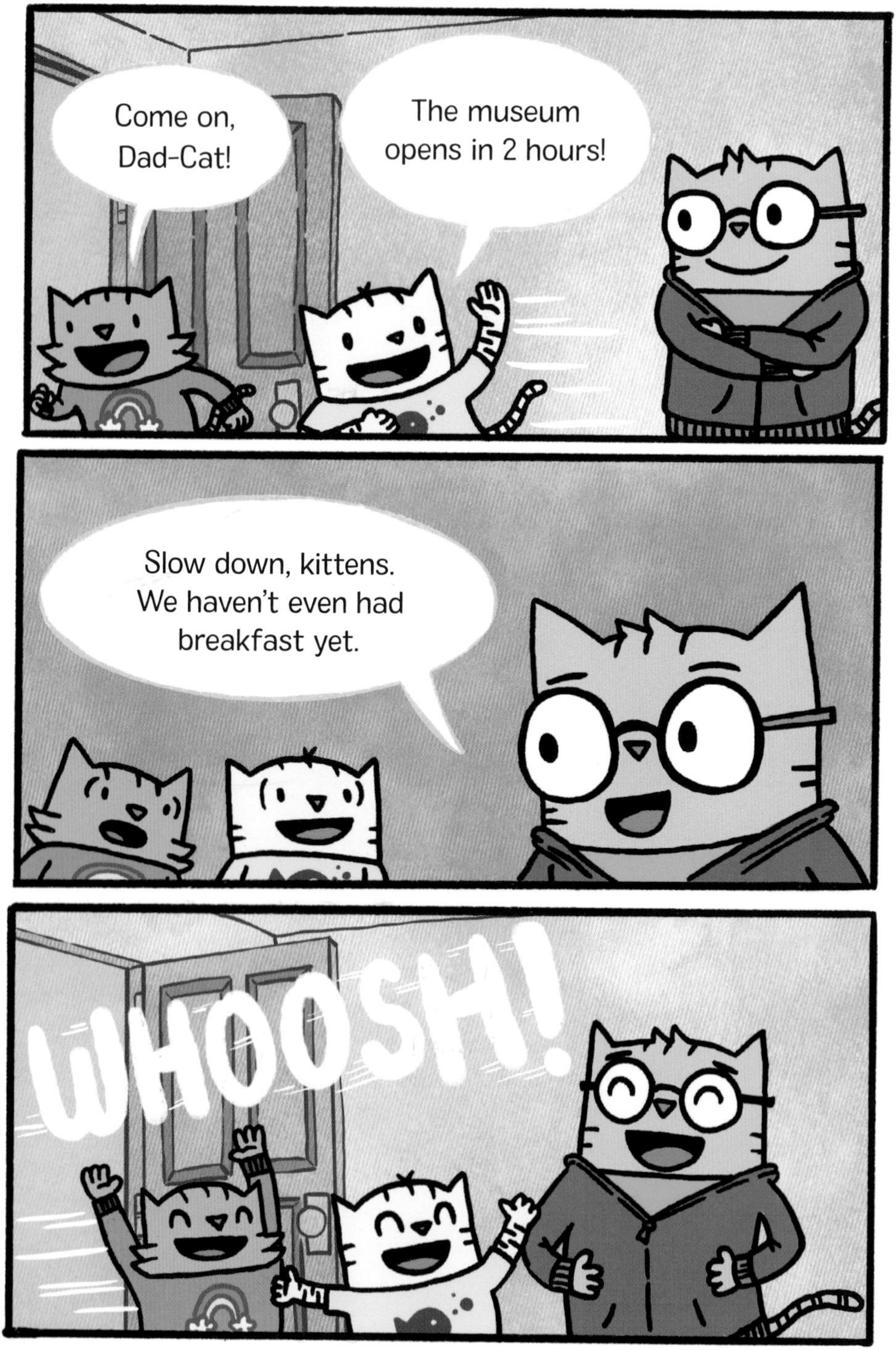
Come on, Dad-Cat!
The museum opens in 2 hours!
Slow down, kittens. We haven't even had breakfast yet.
WHOOSH!

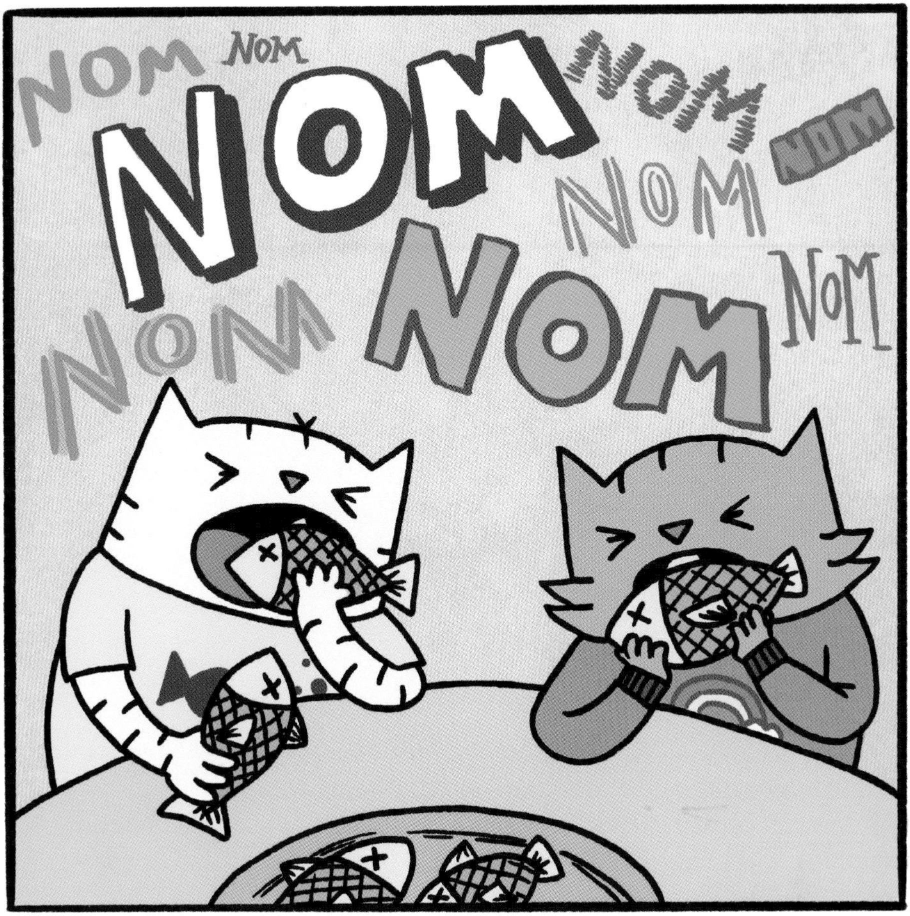
NOM NOM NOM NOM NOM NOM NOM NOM NOM

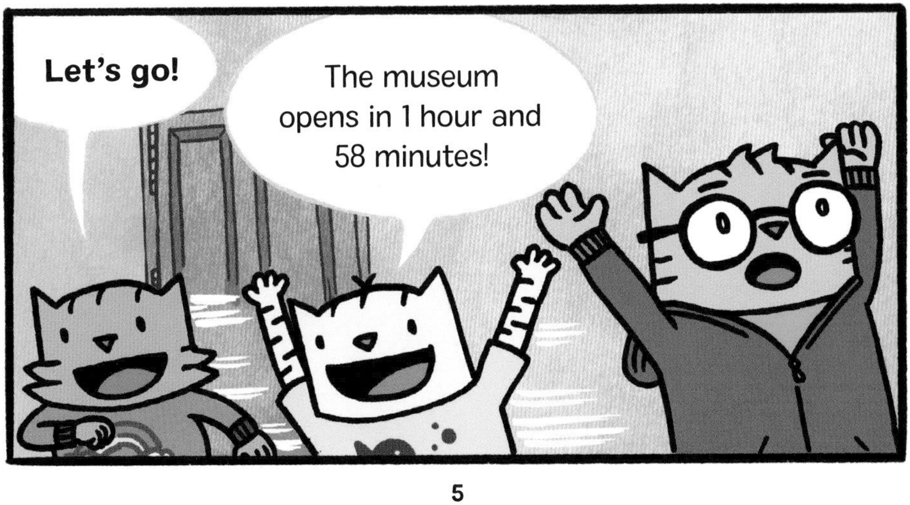
Let's go!
The museum opens in 1 hour and 58 minutes!

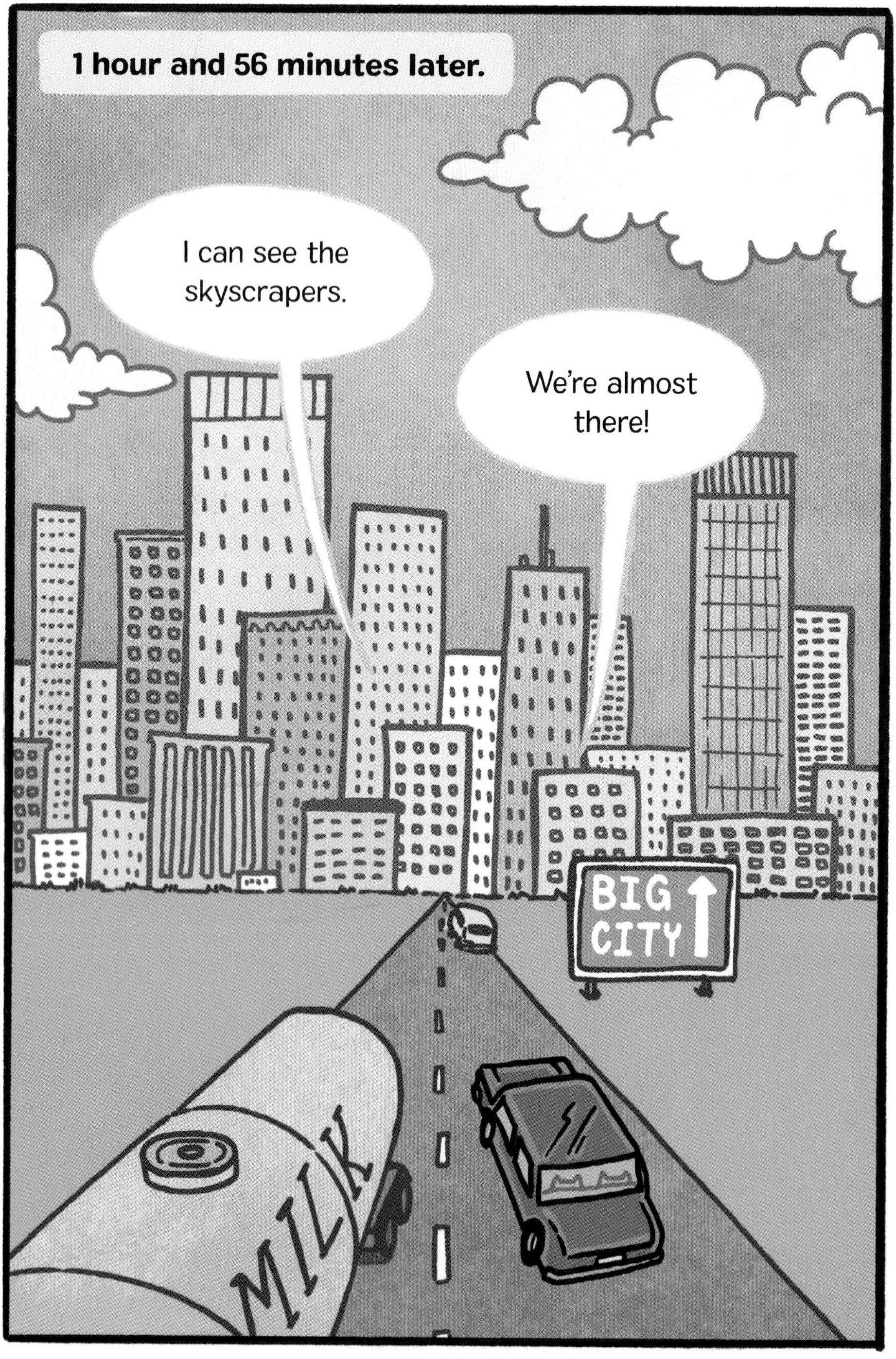
1 hour and 56 minutes later.
I can see the skyscrapers.
We're almost there!
BIG CITY
MILK

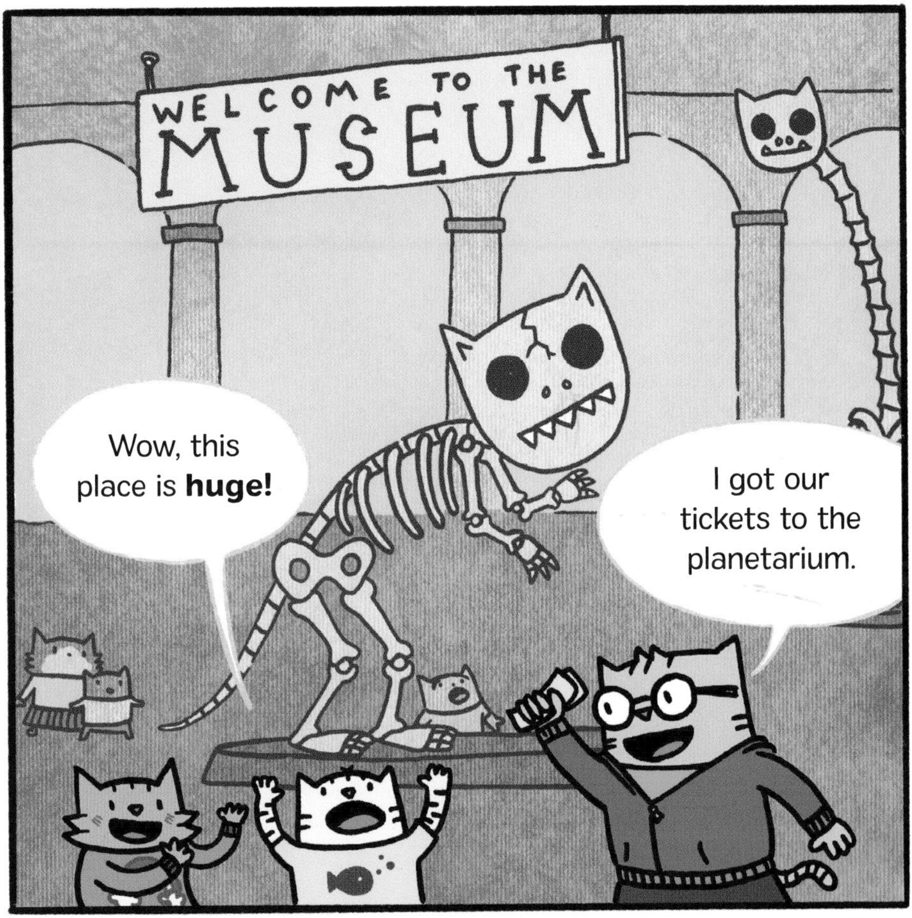
WELCOME TO THE MUSEUM
Wow, this place is **huge!**
I got our tickets to the planetarium.

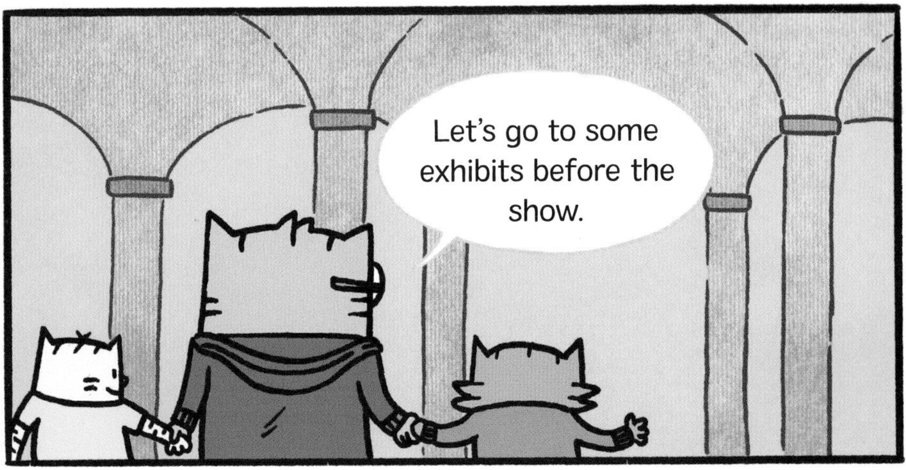
Let's go to some exhibits before the show.

CHAPTER 2

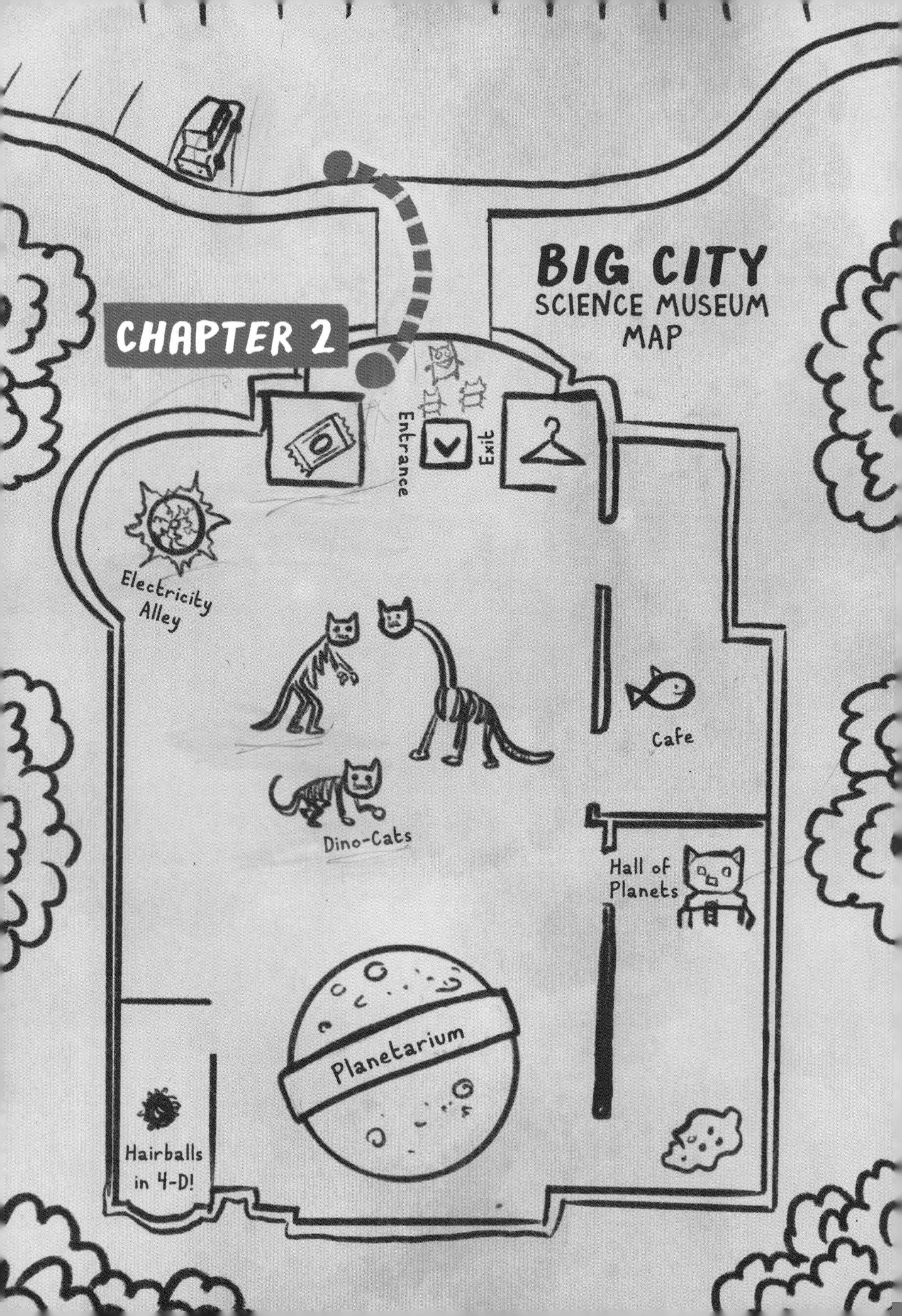
BIG CITY
SCIENCE MUSEUM
MAP
Entrance
Exit
Electricity Alley
Cafe
Dino-Cats
Hall of Planets
Planetarium
Hairballs in 4-D!

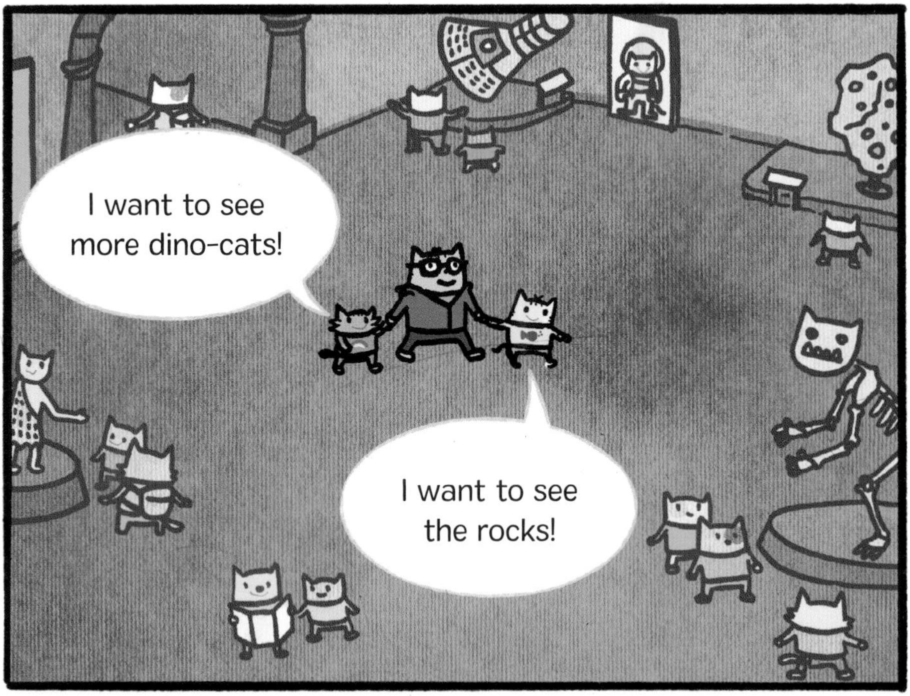
I want to see more dino-cats!
I want to see the rocks!

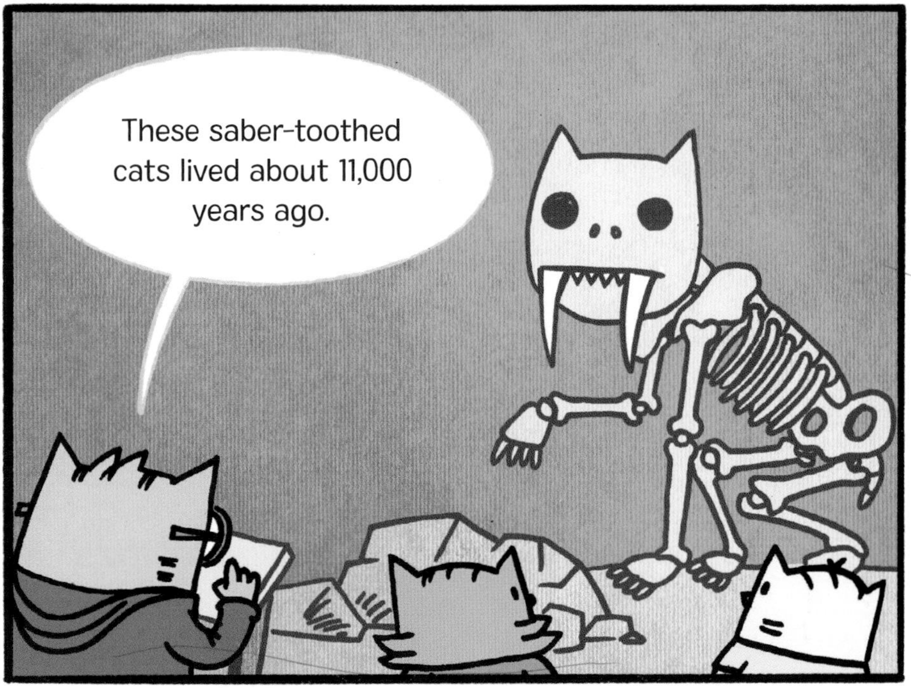
These saber-toothed cats lived about 11,000 years ago.

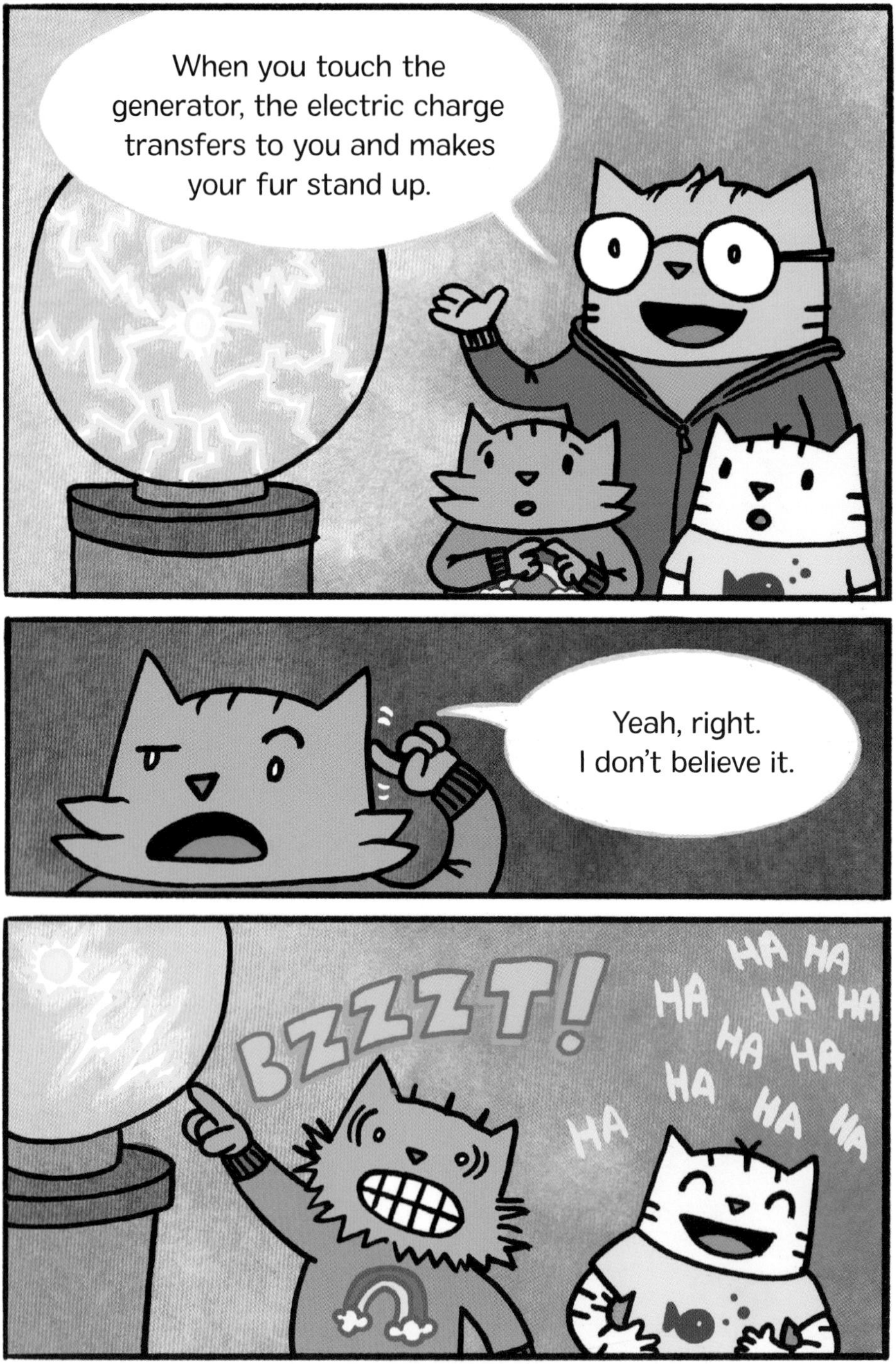
When you touch the generator, the electric charge transfers to you and makes your fur stand up.
Yeah, right. I don't believe it.
BZZZZT!
HA HA HA HA HA HA HA HA HA HA HA HA HA

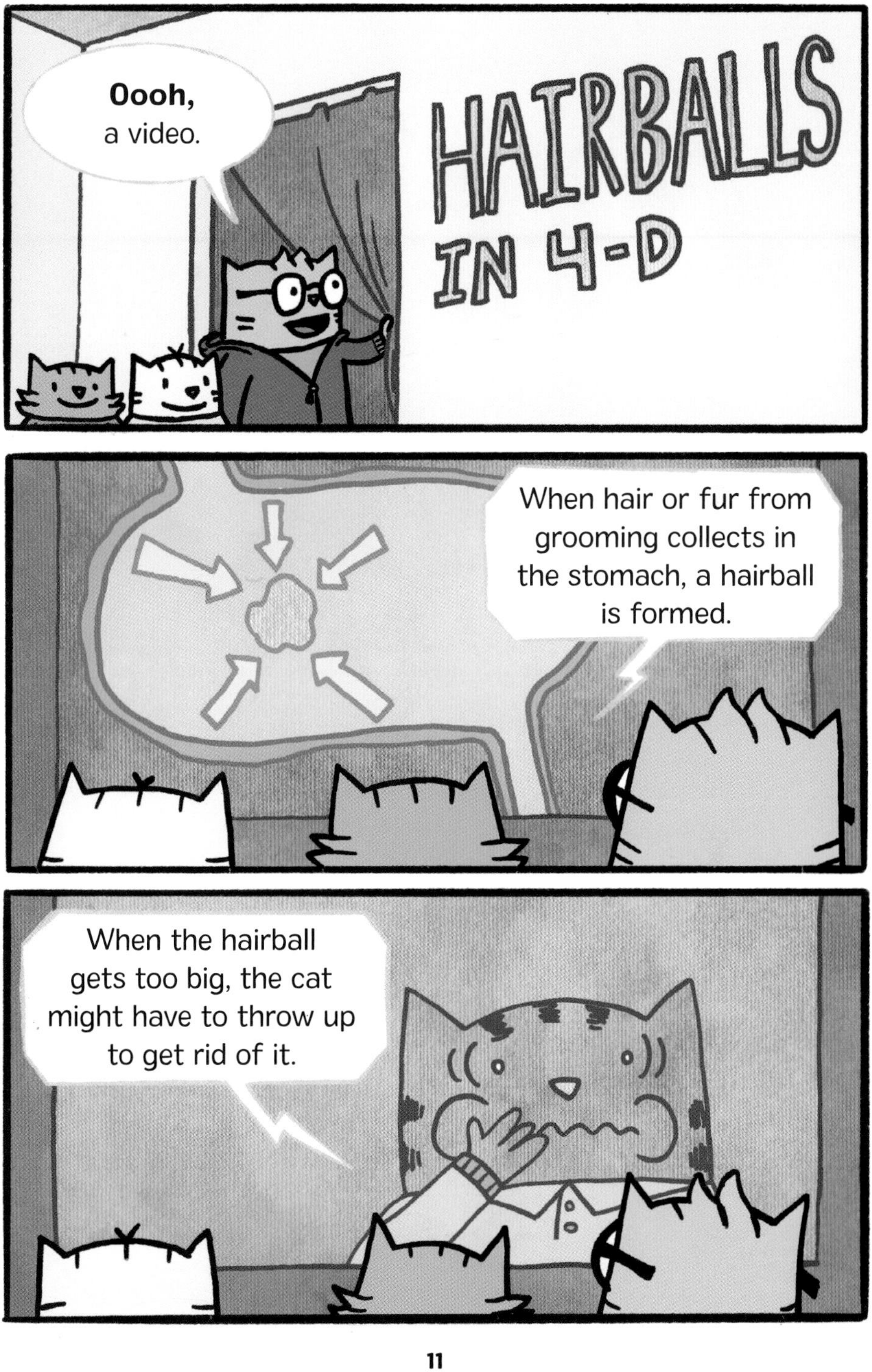
Oooh, a video.
HAIRBALLS IN 4-D
When hair or fur from grooming collects in the stomach, a hairball is formed.
When the hairball gets too big, the cat might have to throw up to get rid of it.

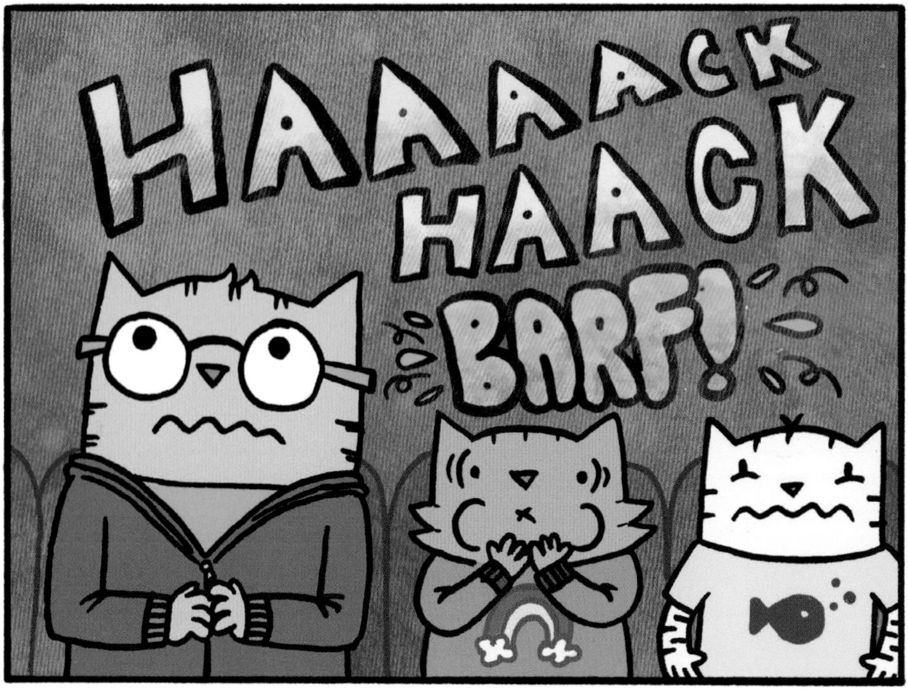
HAAAACK
HAAACK
BARF!

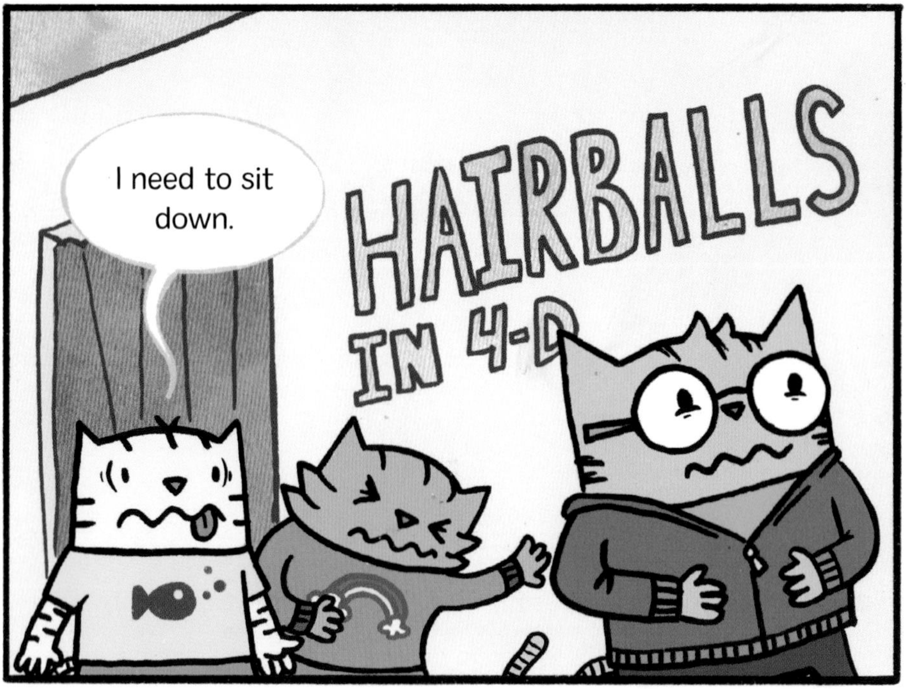
I need to sit down.
HAIRBALLS
IN 4-D

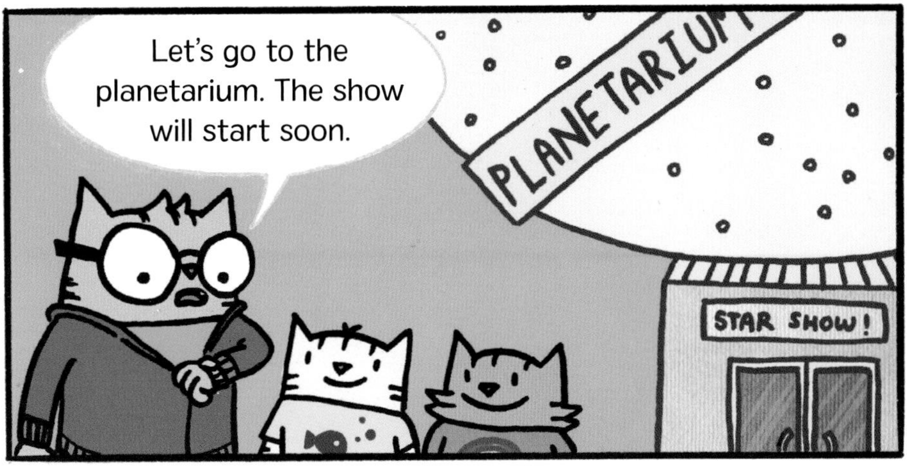
Let's go to the planetarium. The show will start soon.
PLANETARIUM
STAR SHOW!

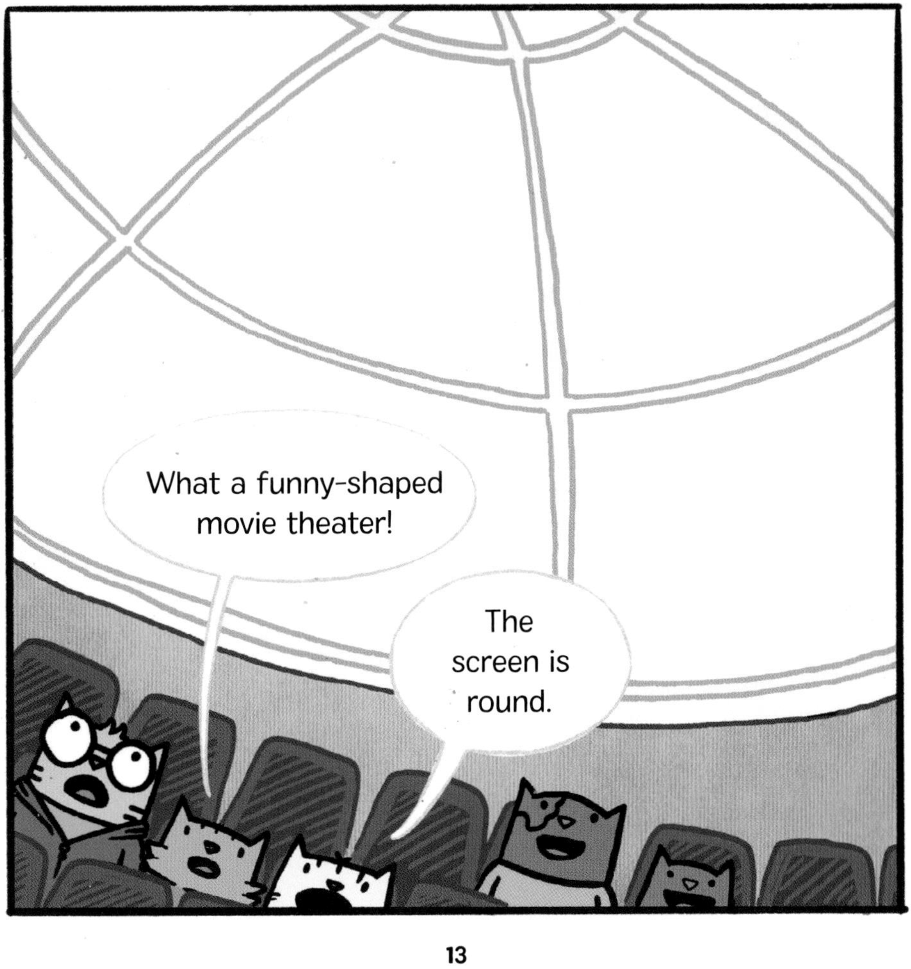
What a funny-shaped movie theater!
The screen is round.

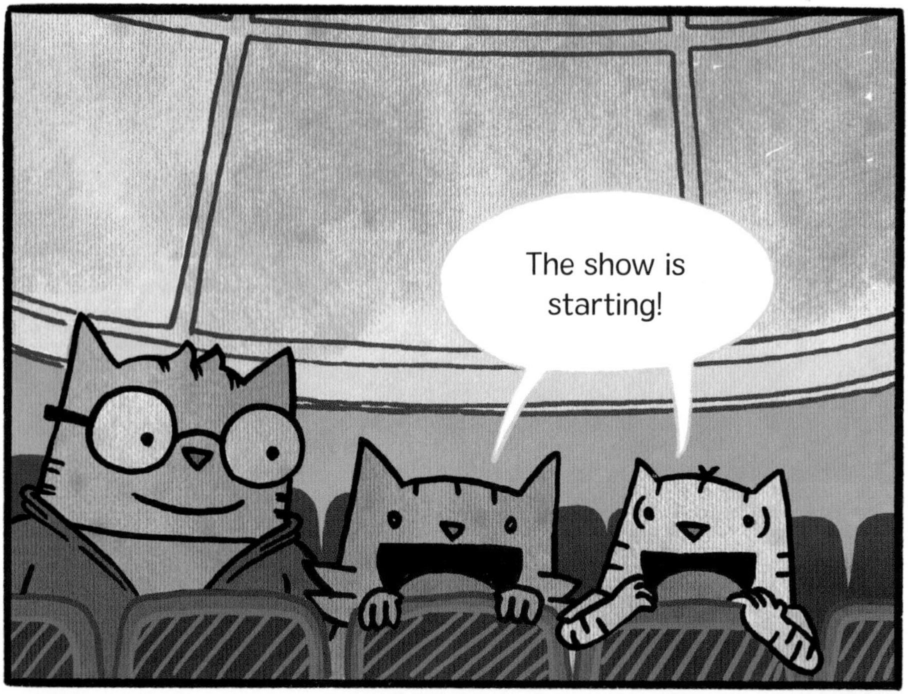
The show is starting!

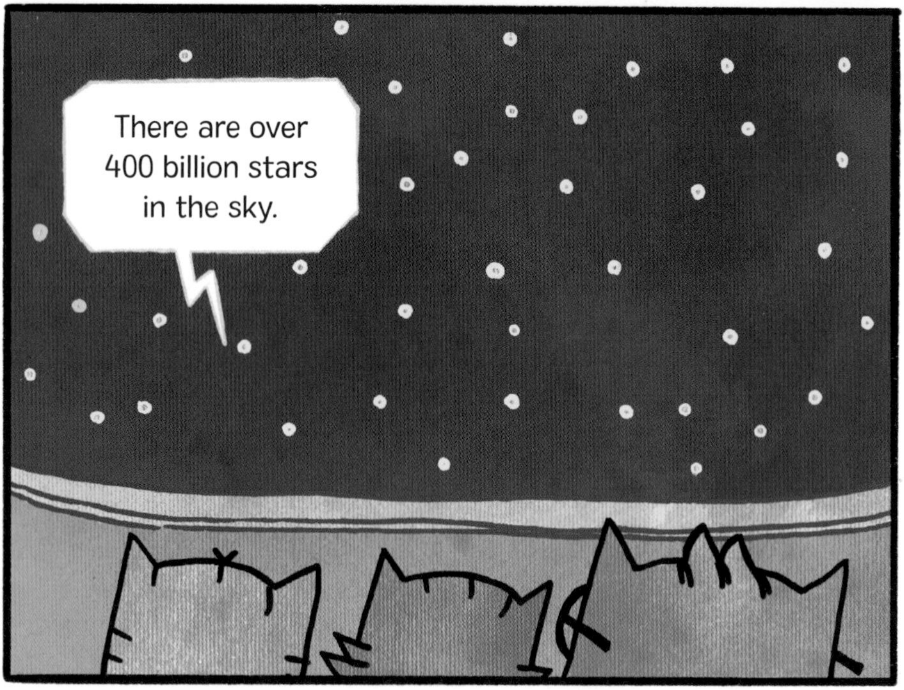
There are over 400 billion stars in the sky.

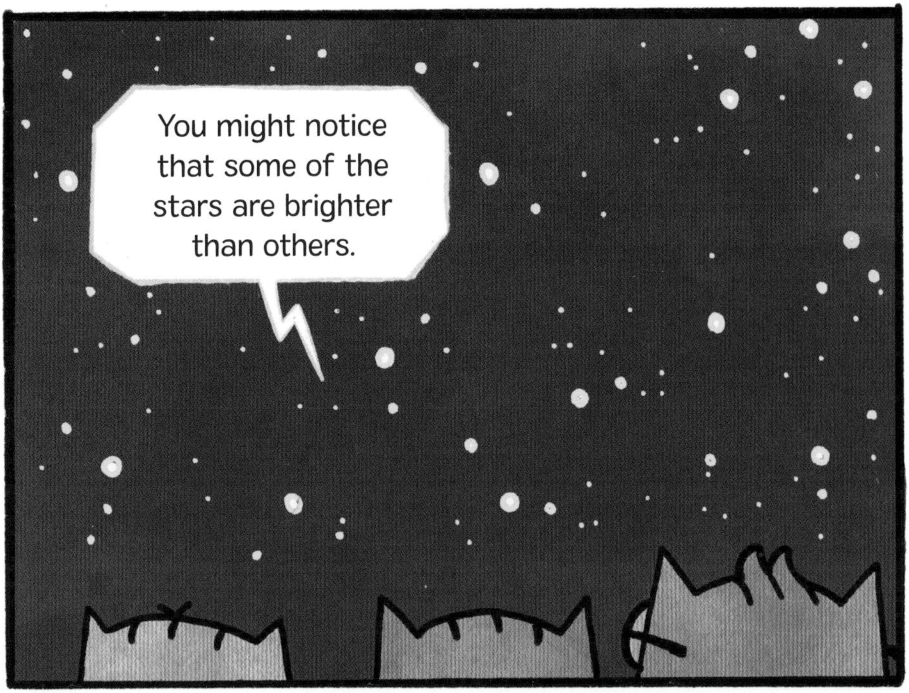
You might notice that some of the stars are brighter than others.

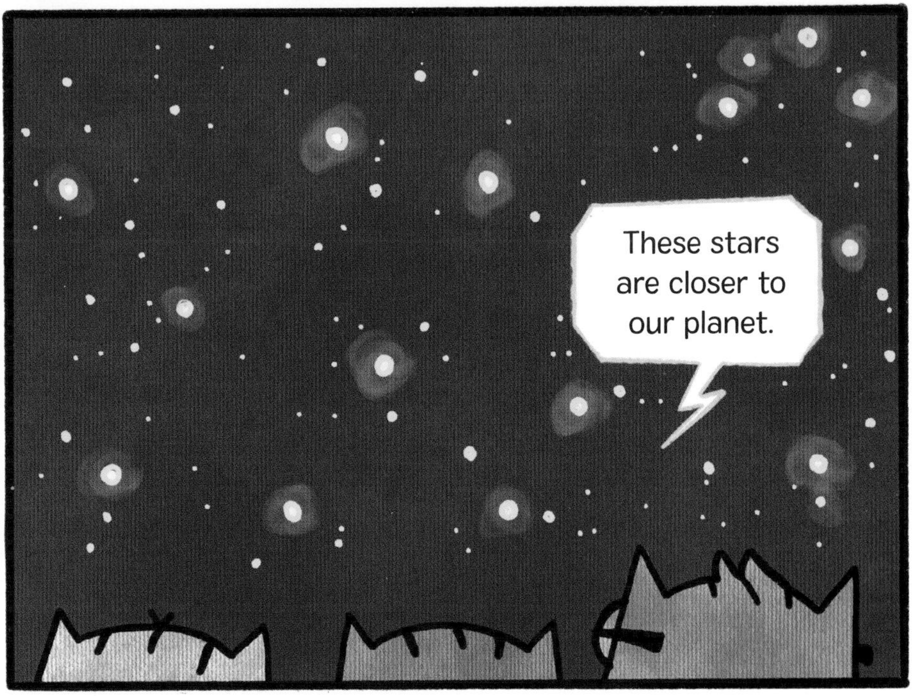
These stars are closer to our planet.

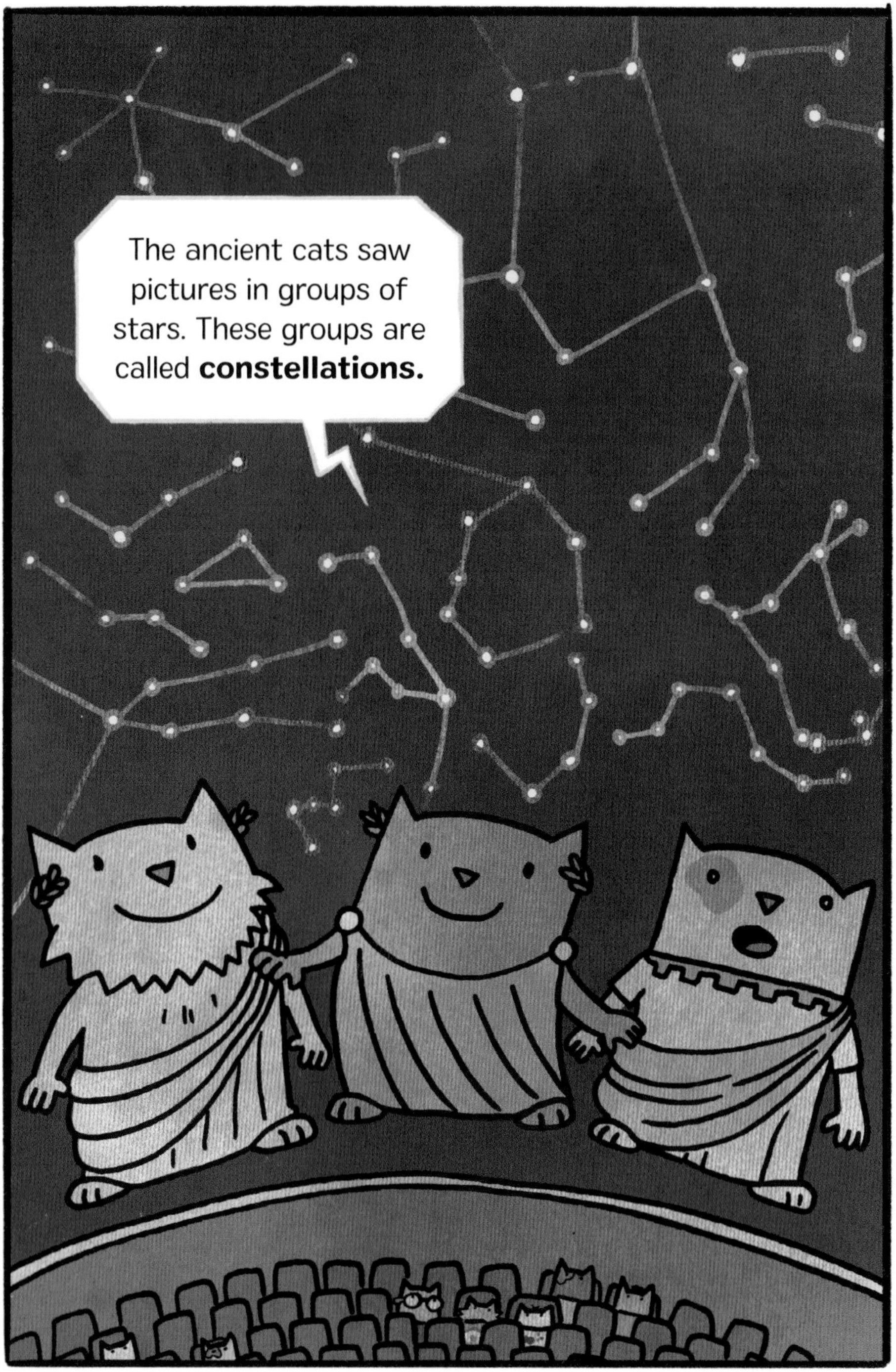
The ancient cats saw pictures in groups of stars. These groups are called **constellations.**

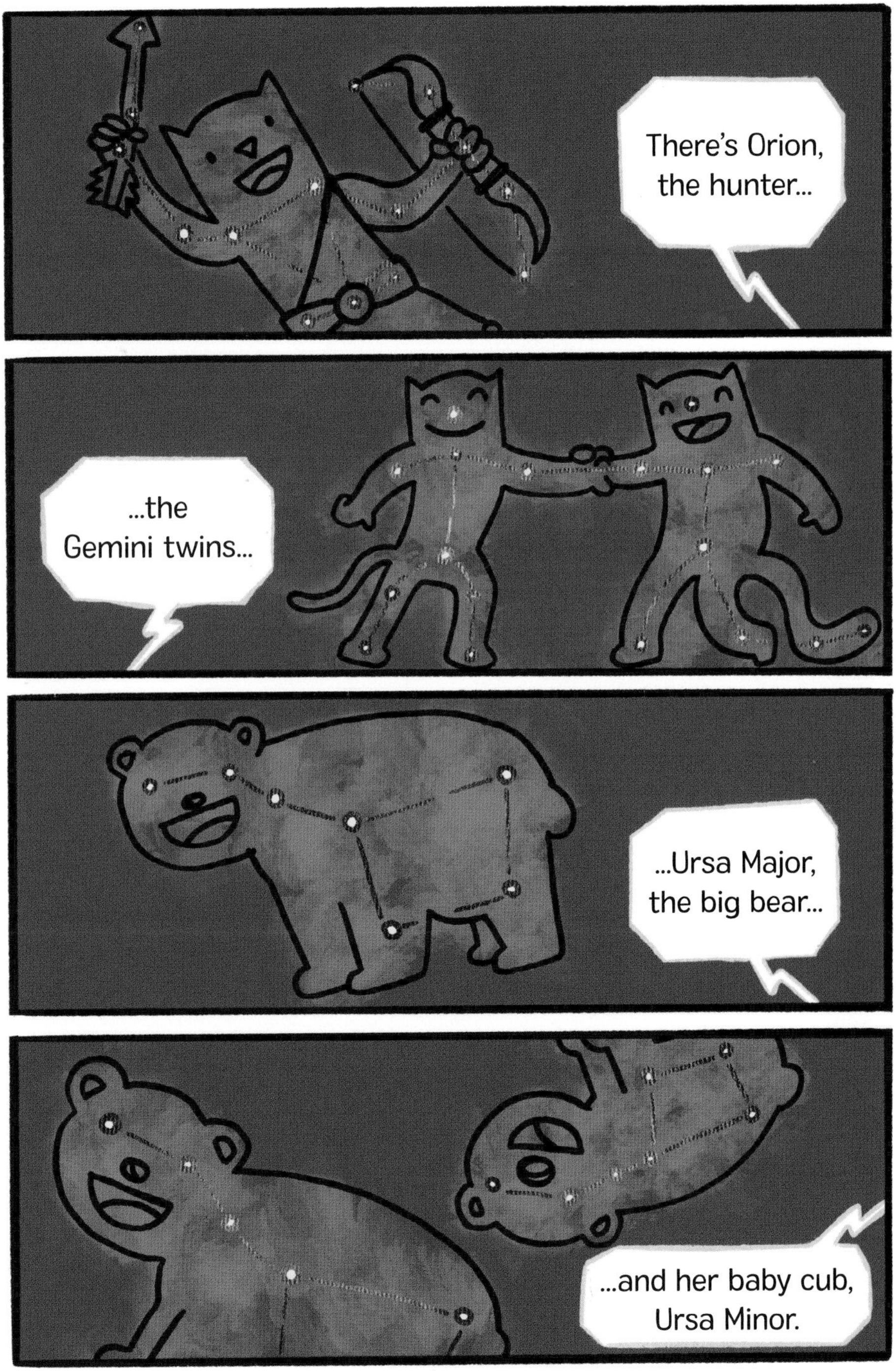
There's Orion, the hunter...
...the Gemini twins...
...Ursa Major, the big bear...
...and her baby cub, Ursa Minor.

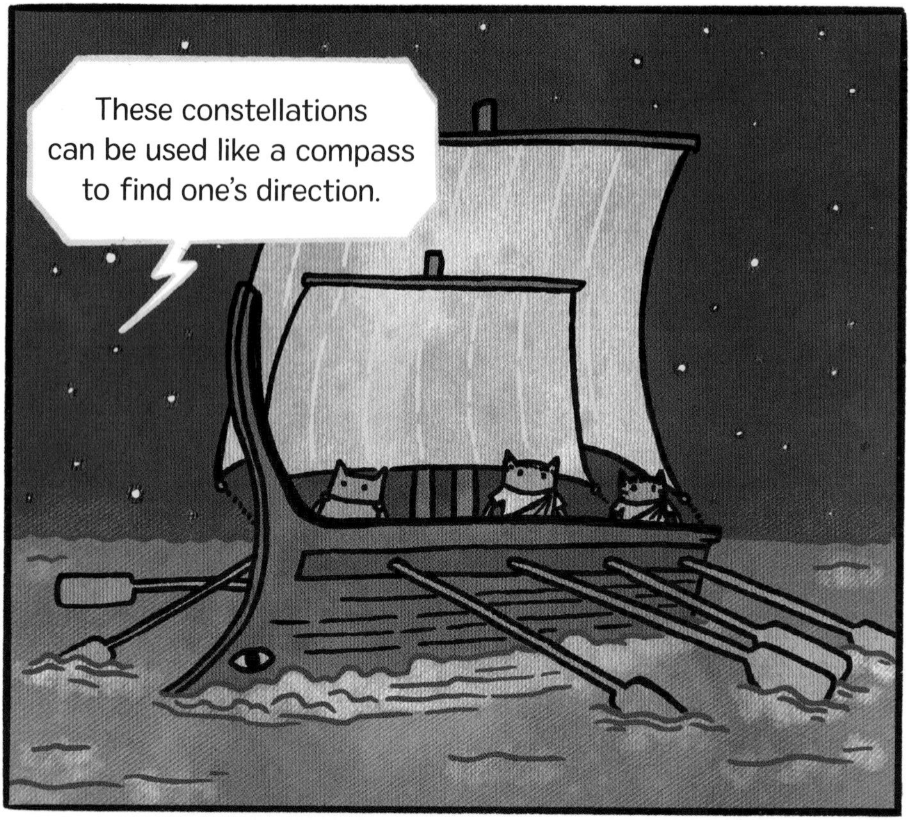
These constellations can be used like a compass to find one's direction.

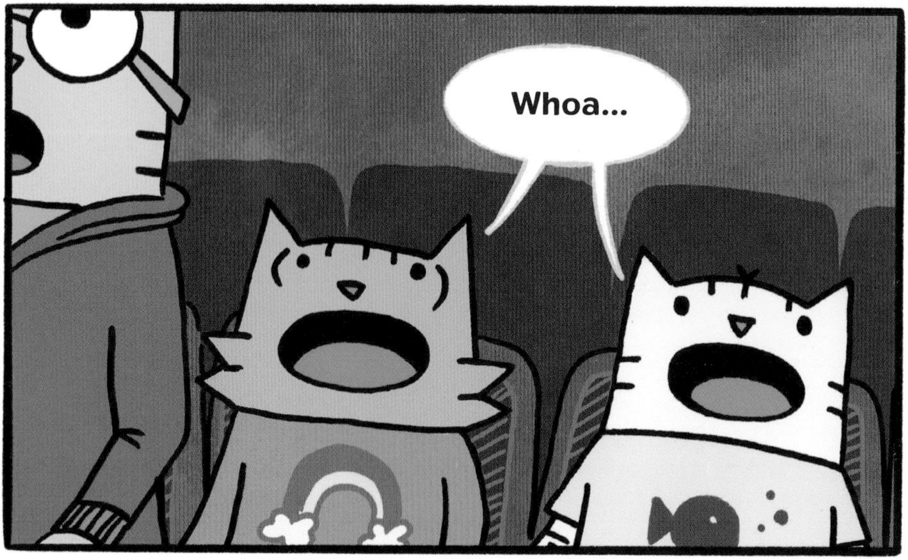
Whoa...

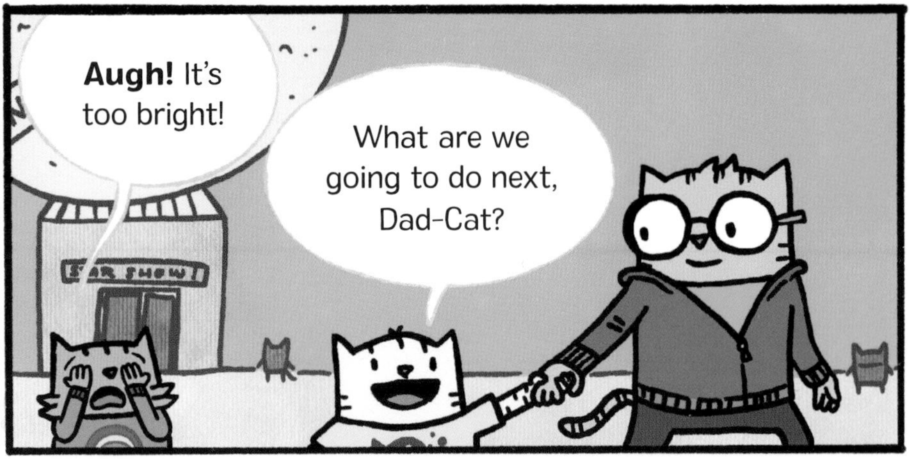
Augh! It's too bright!
What are we going to do next, Dad-Cat?

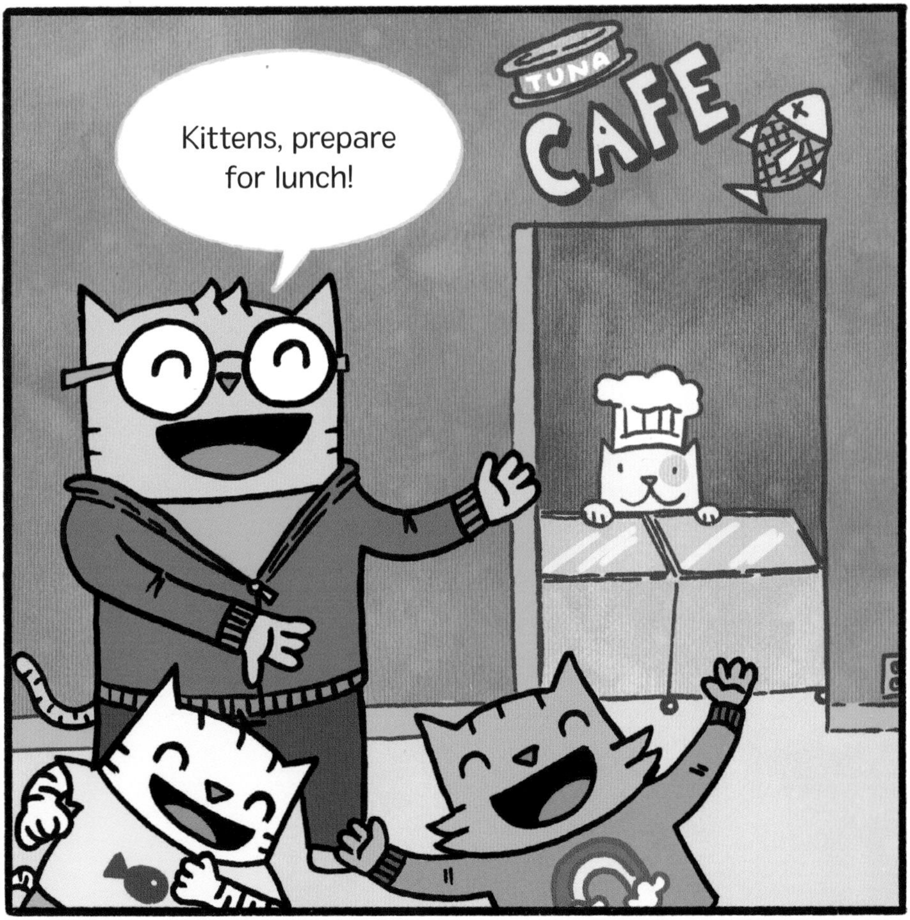
TUNA
CAFE
Kittens, prepare for lunch!

CHAPTER 3

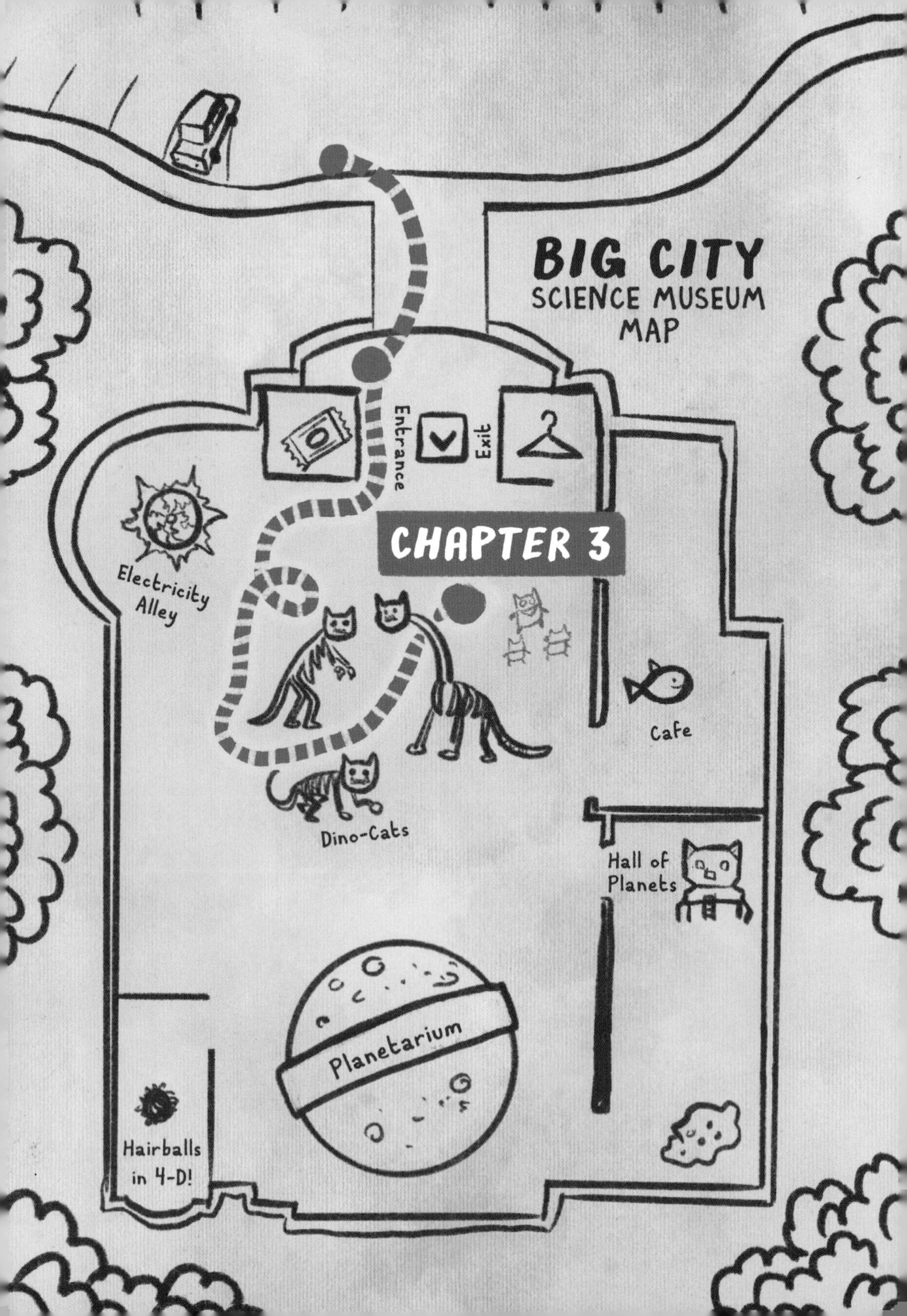
BIG CITY
SCIENCE MUSEUM
MAP
Entrance
Exit
Electricity Alley
Dino-Cats
Cafe
Hall of Planets
Planetarium
Hairballs in 4-D!

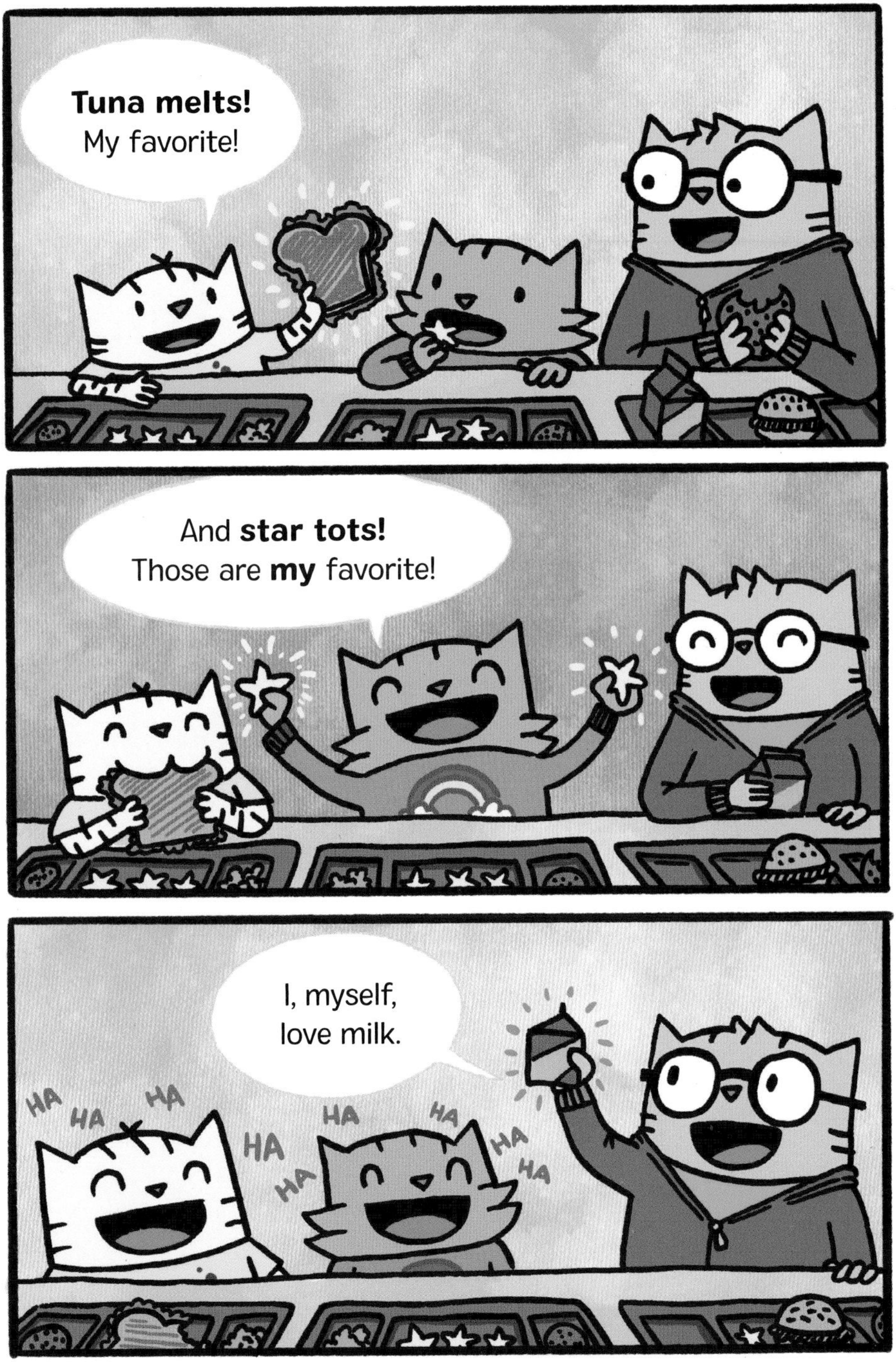
Tuna melts! My favorite!
And **star tots!** Those are **my** favorite!
I, myself, love milk.
HA HA HA HA HA HA HA HA HA

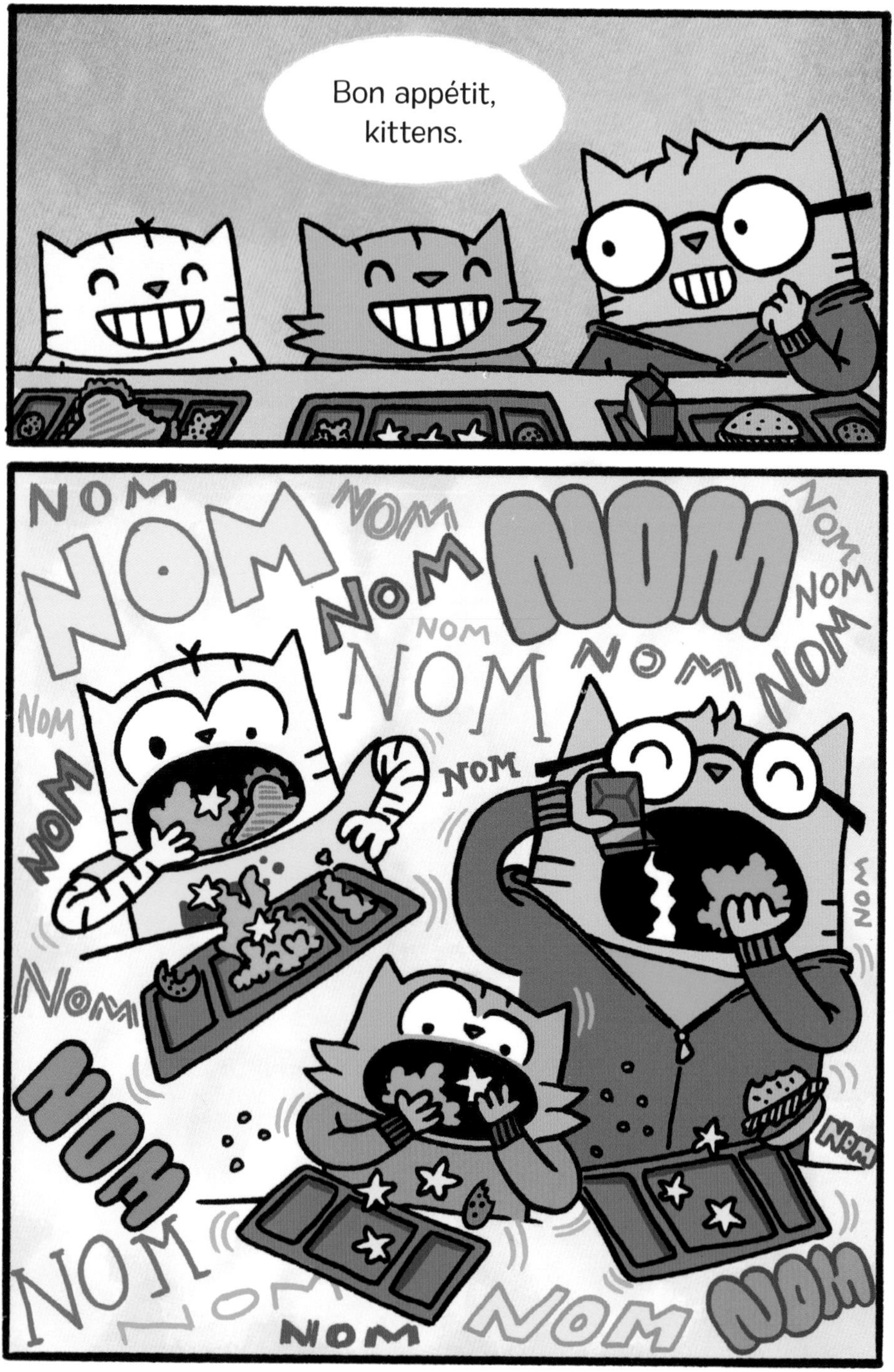
Bon appétit, kittens.
NOM
NOM
NOM
NOM
NOM
NOM
NOM
NOM
NOM
NOM
NOM
NOM
NOM
NOM
NOM
NOM
NOM
NOM
NOM
NOM
NOM
NOM
NOM

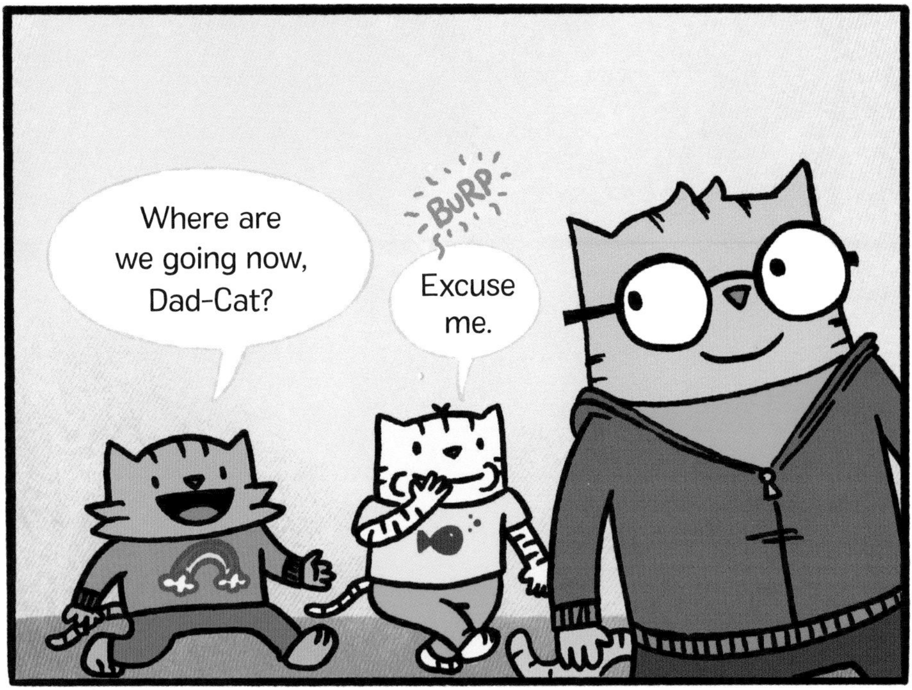
Where are we going now, Dad-Cat?
BURP
Excuse me.

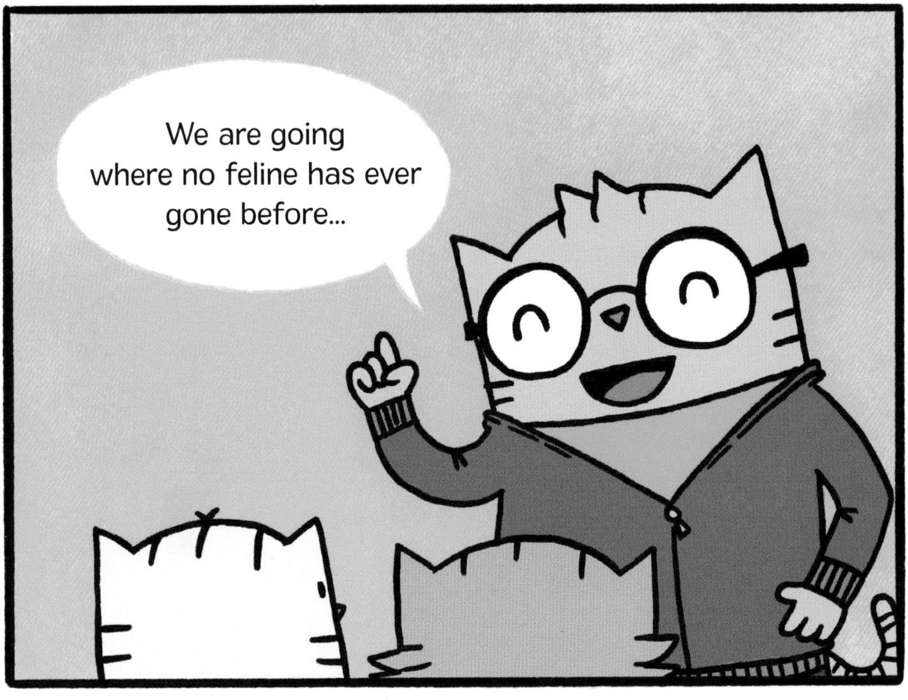
We are going where no feline has ever gone before...

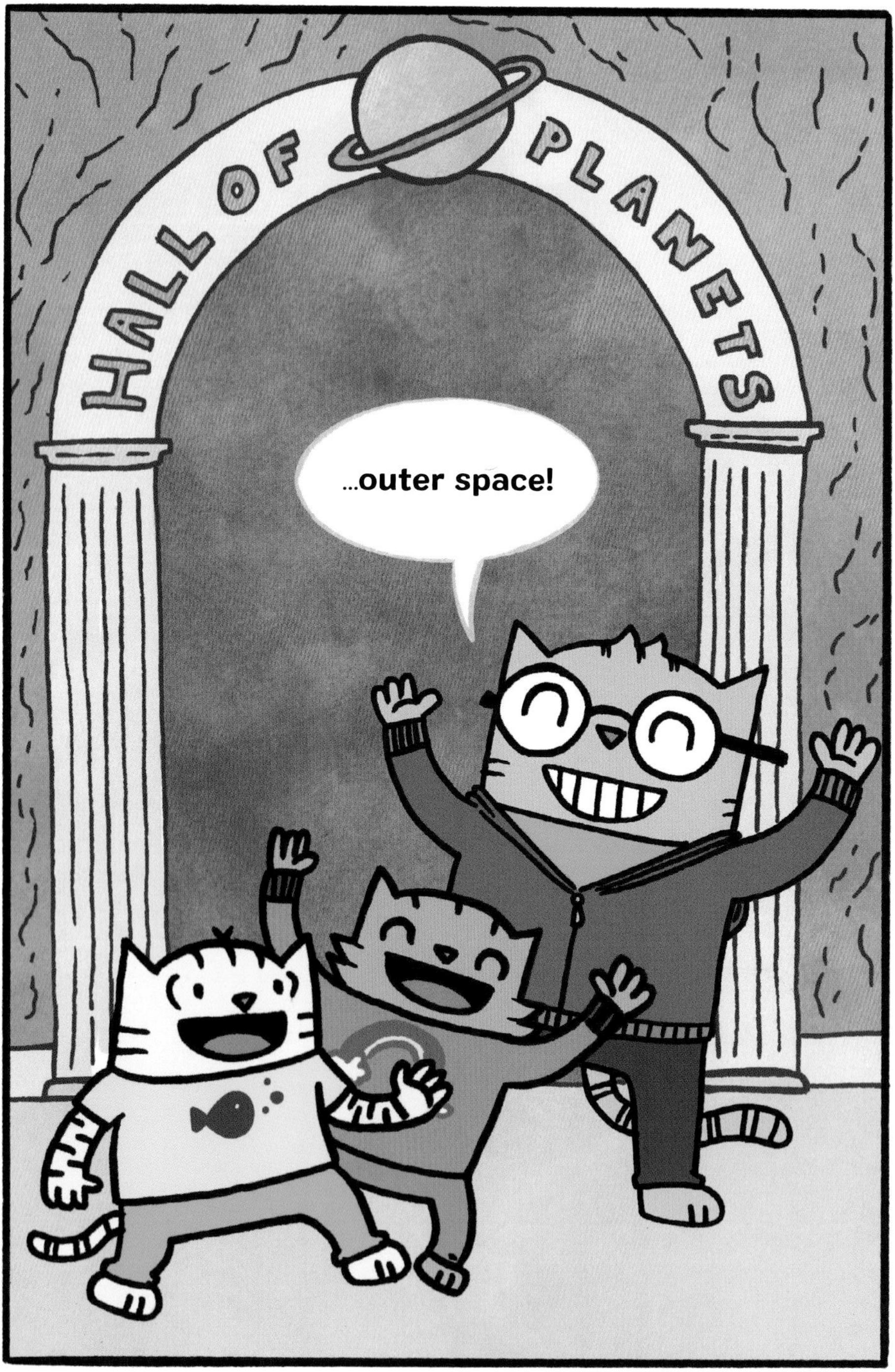
HALL OF PLANETS
...outer space!

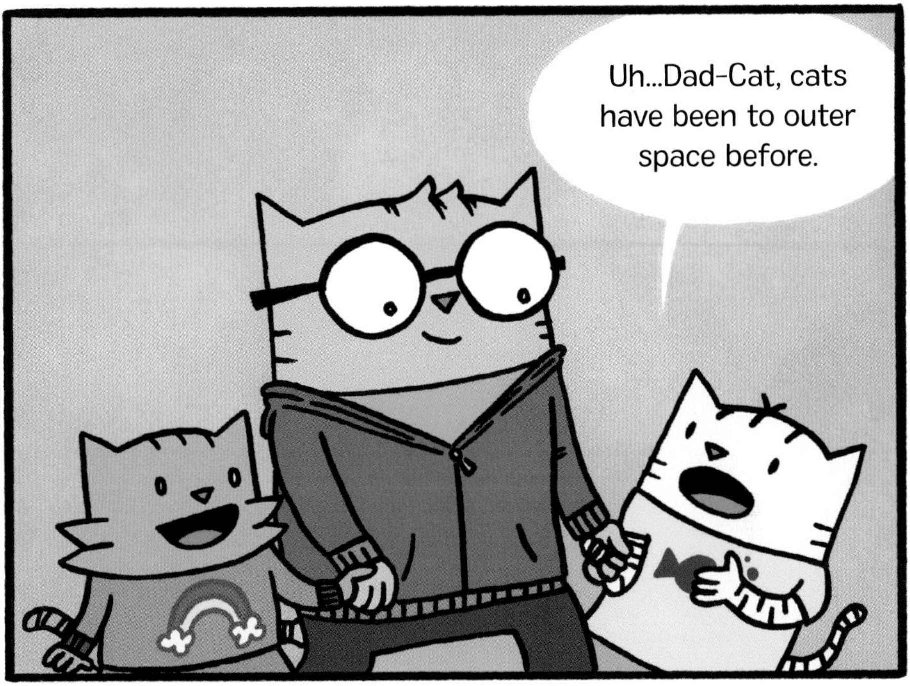
Uh...Dad-Cat, cats have been to outer space before.

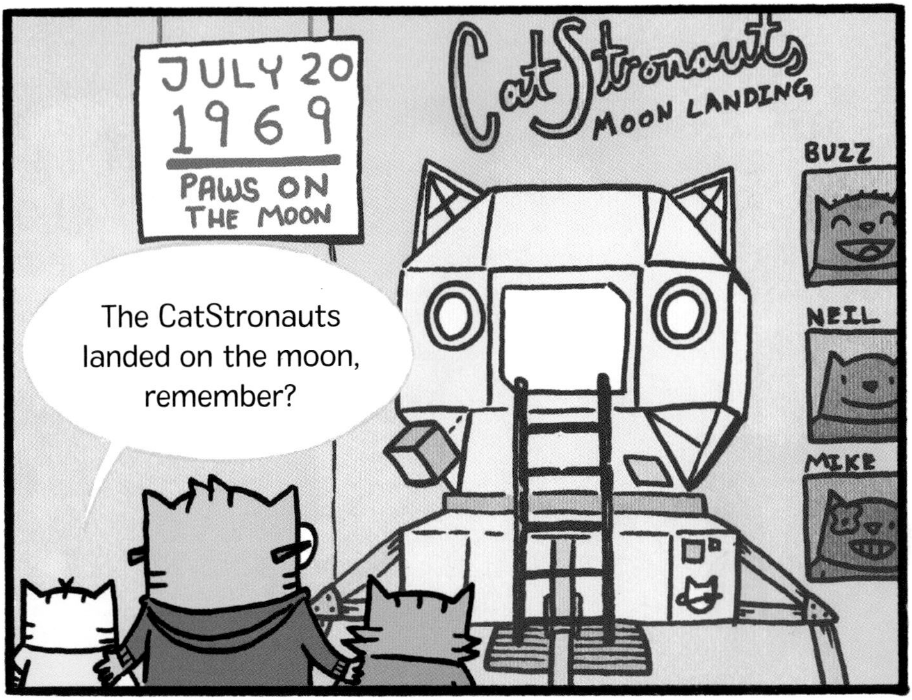
JULY 20
1969
PAWS ON THE MOON
CatStronauts
MOON LANDING
BUZZ
NEIL
MIKE
The CatStronauts landed on the moon, remember?

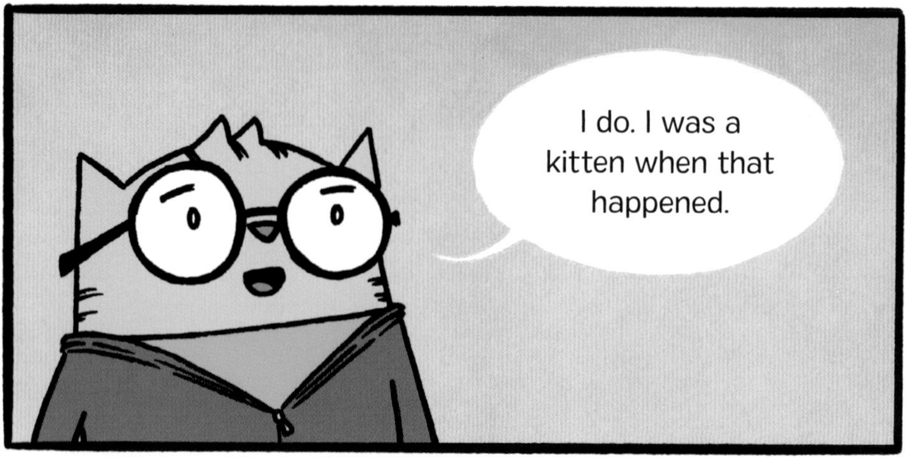
I do. I was a kitten when that happened.

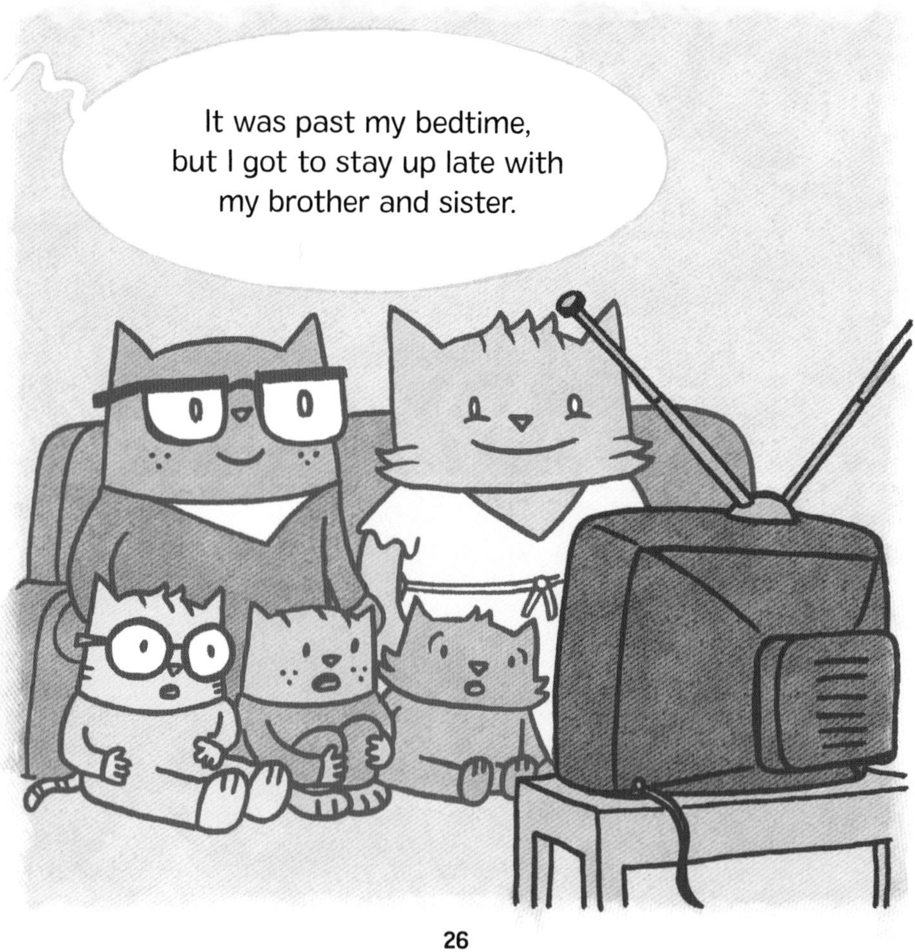
It was past my bedtime, but I got to stay up late with my brother and sister.

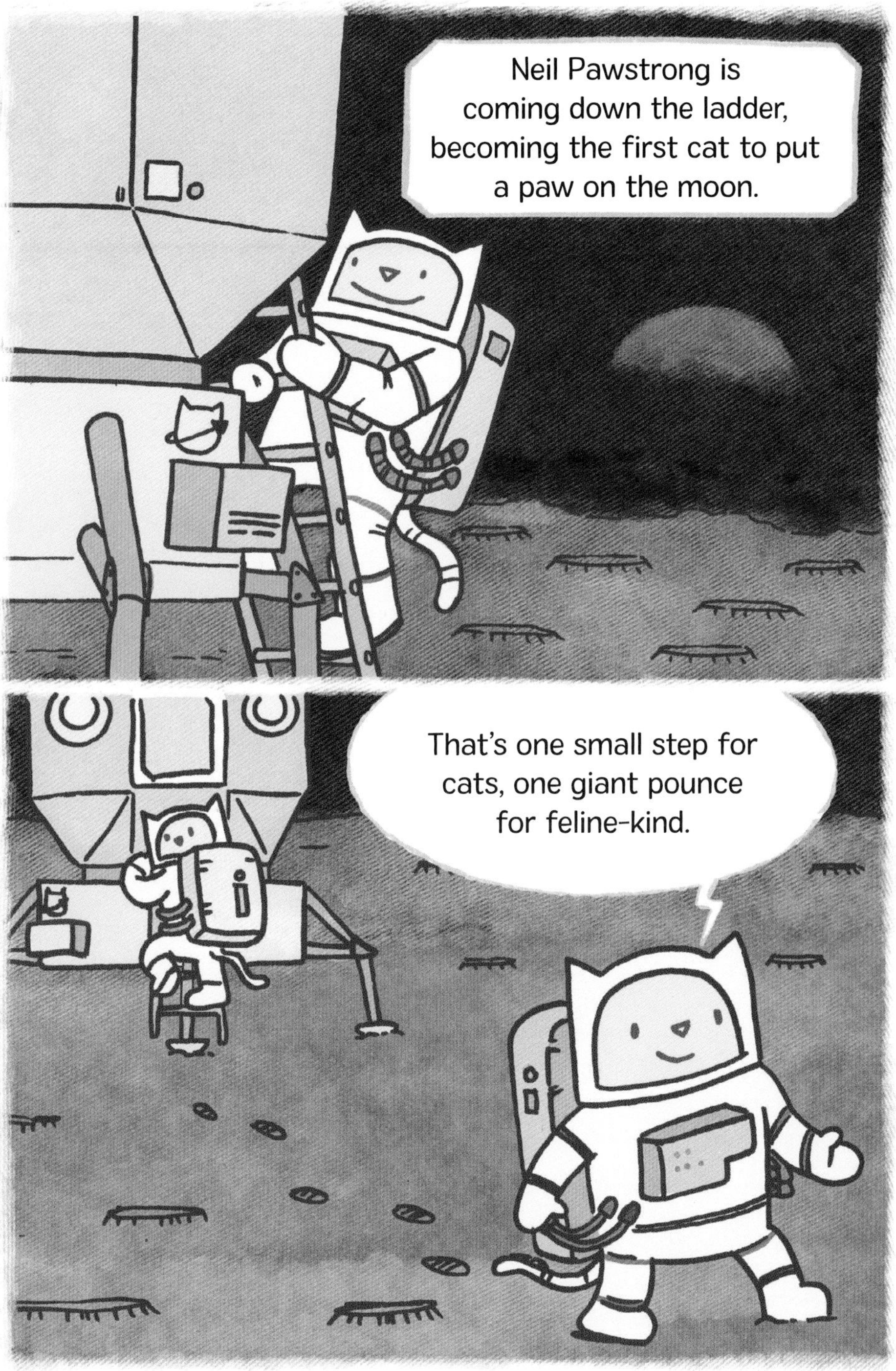
Neil Pawstrong is coming down the ladder, becoming the first cat to put a paw on the moon.
That's one small step for cats, one giant pounce for feline-kind.

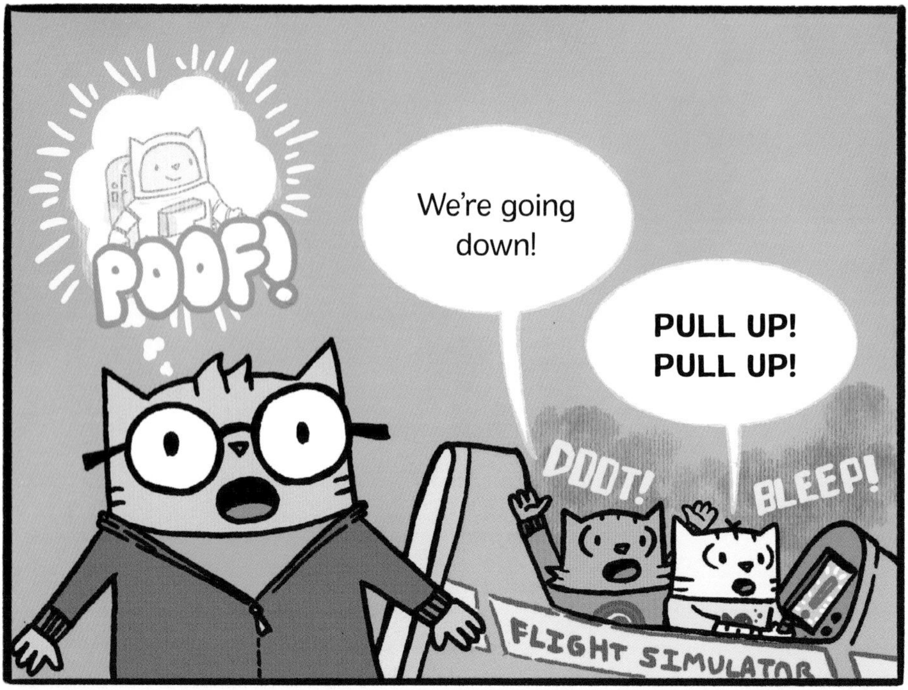
POOF!
We're going down!
PULL UP!
PULL UP!
DOOT!
BLEEP!
FLIGHT SIMULATOR

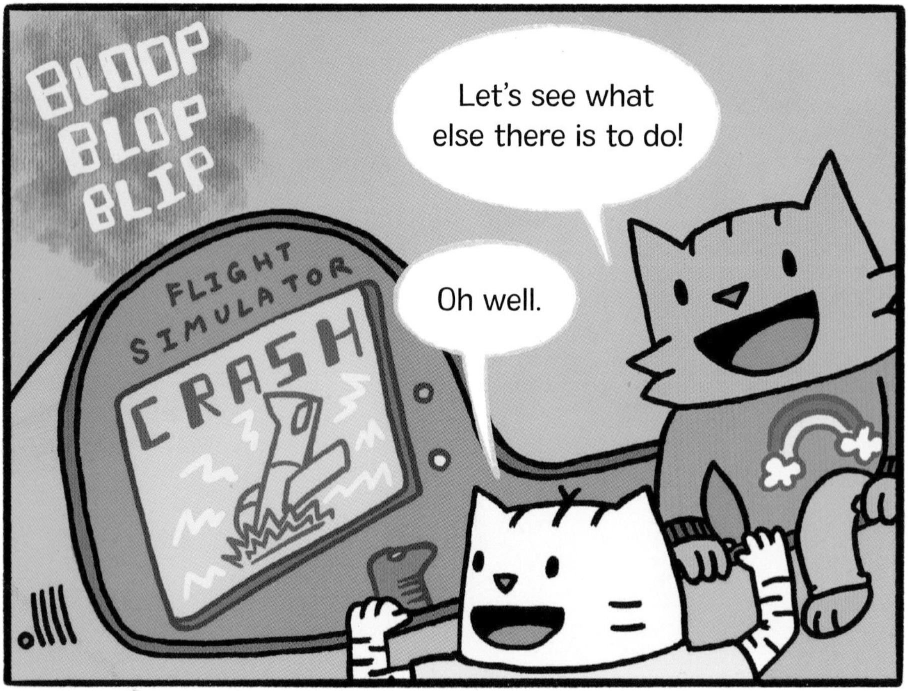
BLOOP
BLOP
BLIP
Let's see what else there is to do!
Oh well.
FLIGHT SIMULATOR
CRASH

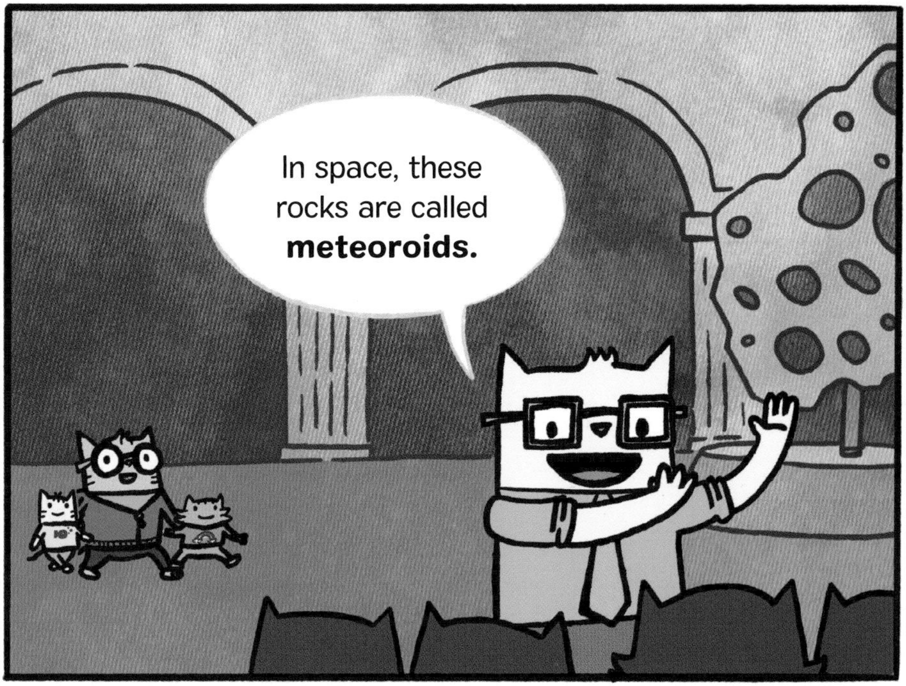
In space, these rocks are called **meteoroids.**

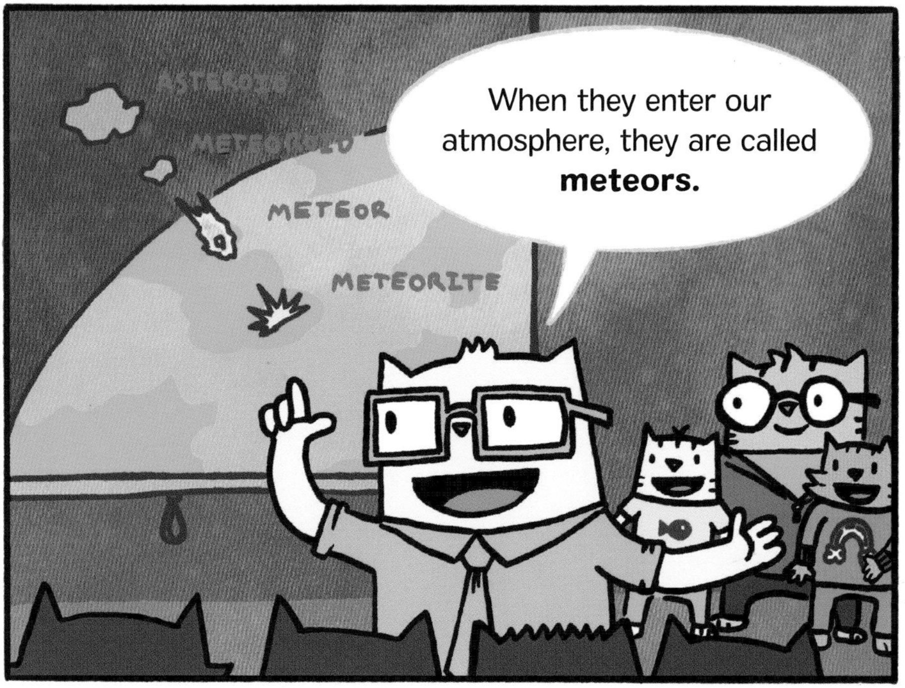
METEOR
METEORITE
When they enter our atmosphere, they are called **meteors.**

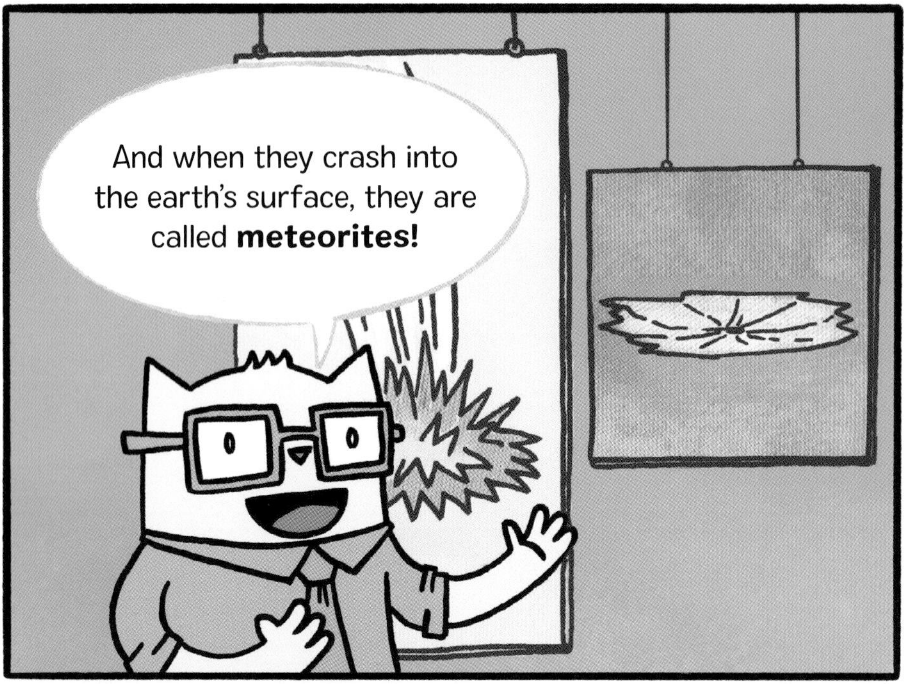
And when they crash into the earth's surface, they are called **meteorites!**

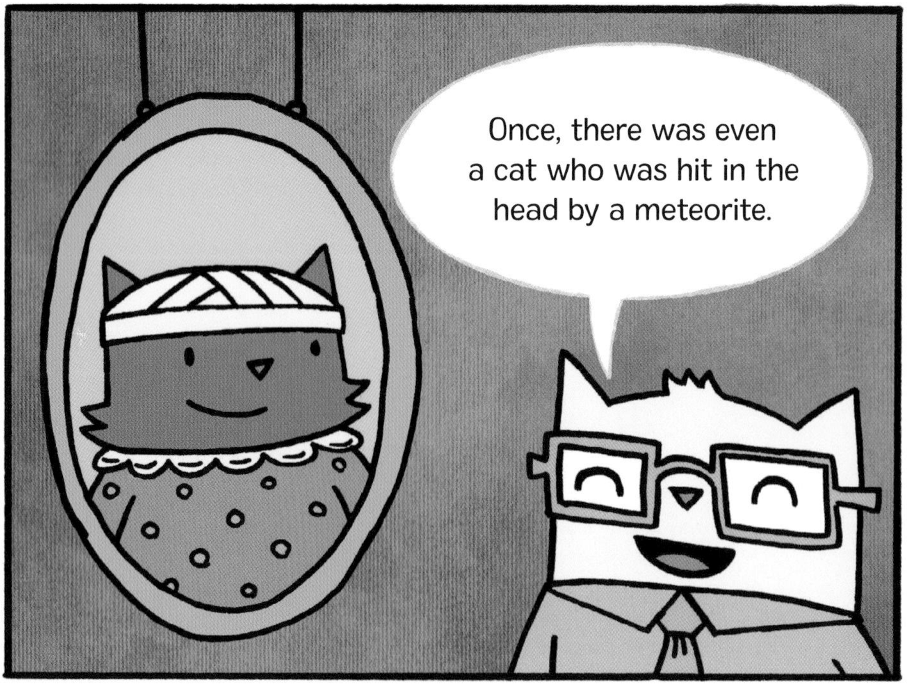
Once, there was even a cat who was hit in the head by a meteorite.

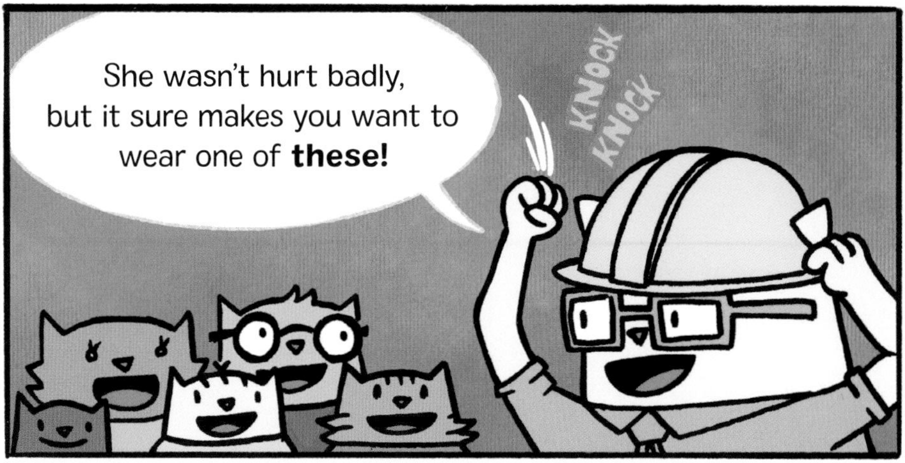
She wasn't hurt badly, but it sure makes you want to wear one of **these!**
KNOCK KNOCK

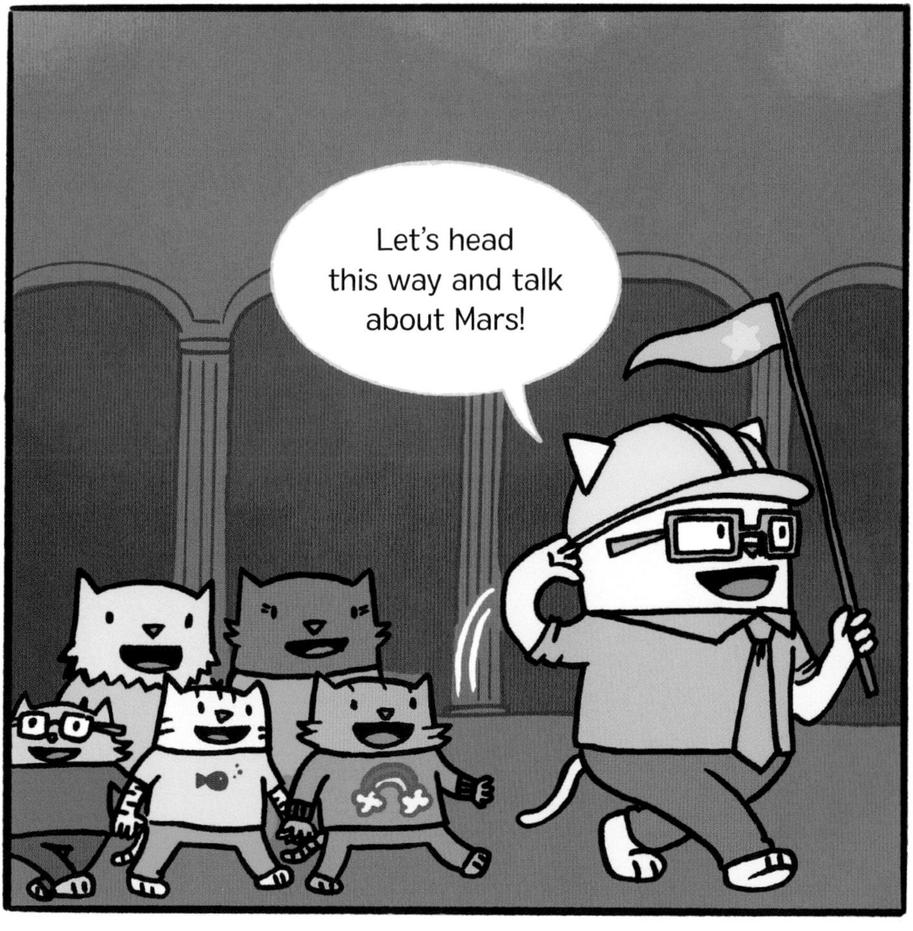
Let's head this way and talk about Mars!

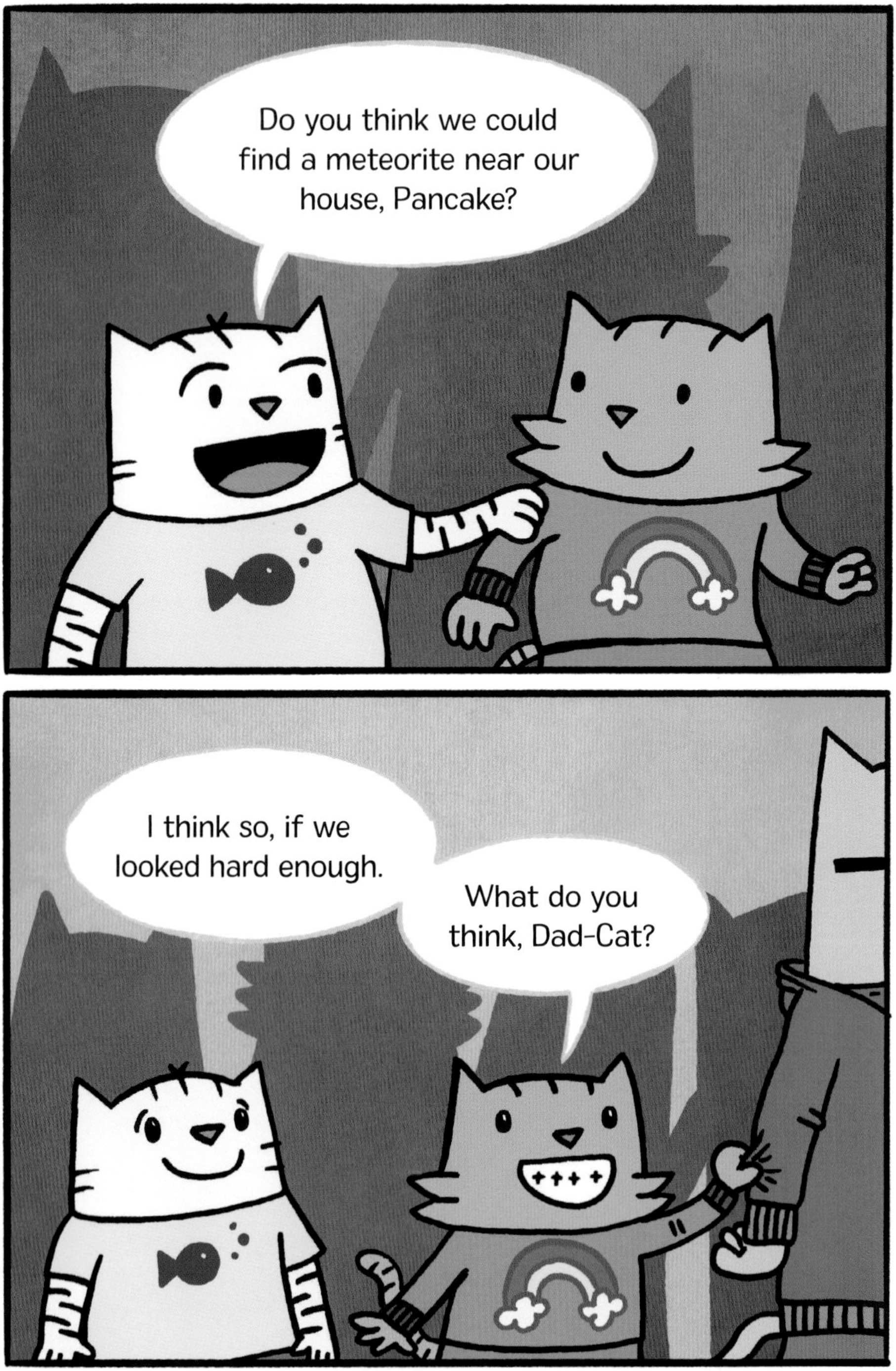
Do you think we could find a meteorite near our house, Pancake?
I think so, if we looked hard enough.
What do you think, Dad-Cat?

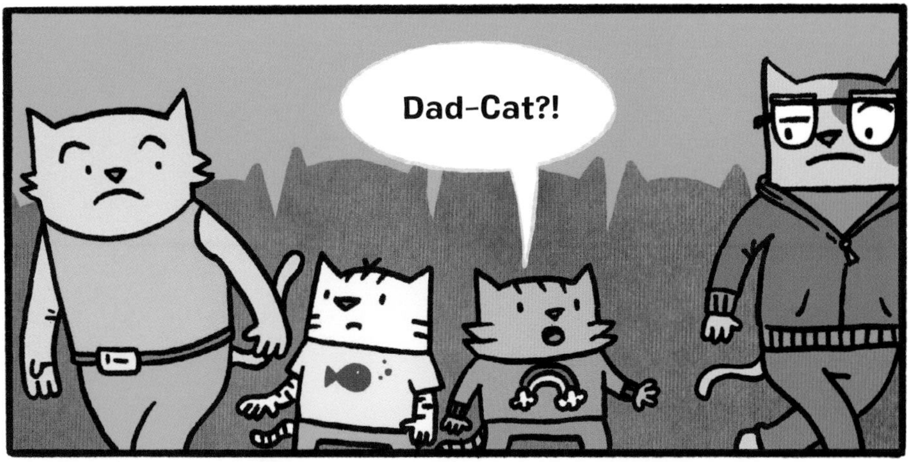
Dad-Cat?!

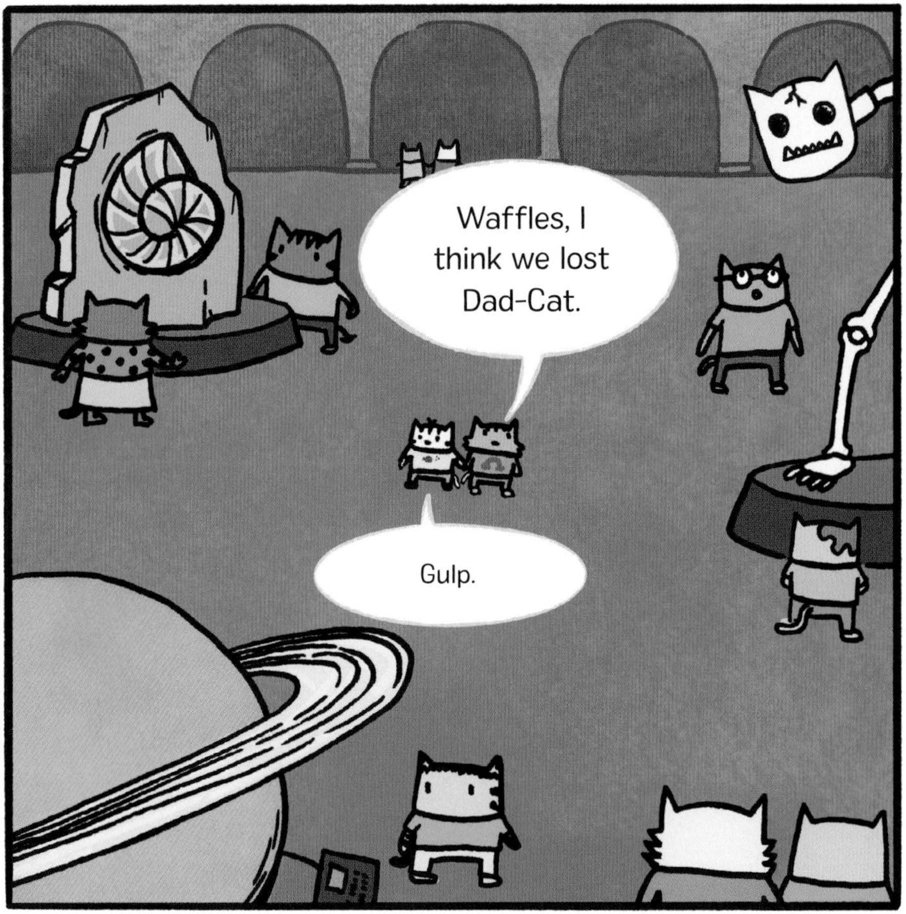
Waffles, I think we lost Dad-Cat.
Gulp.

CHAPTER 4

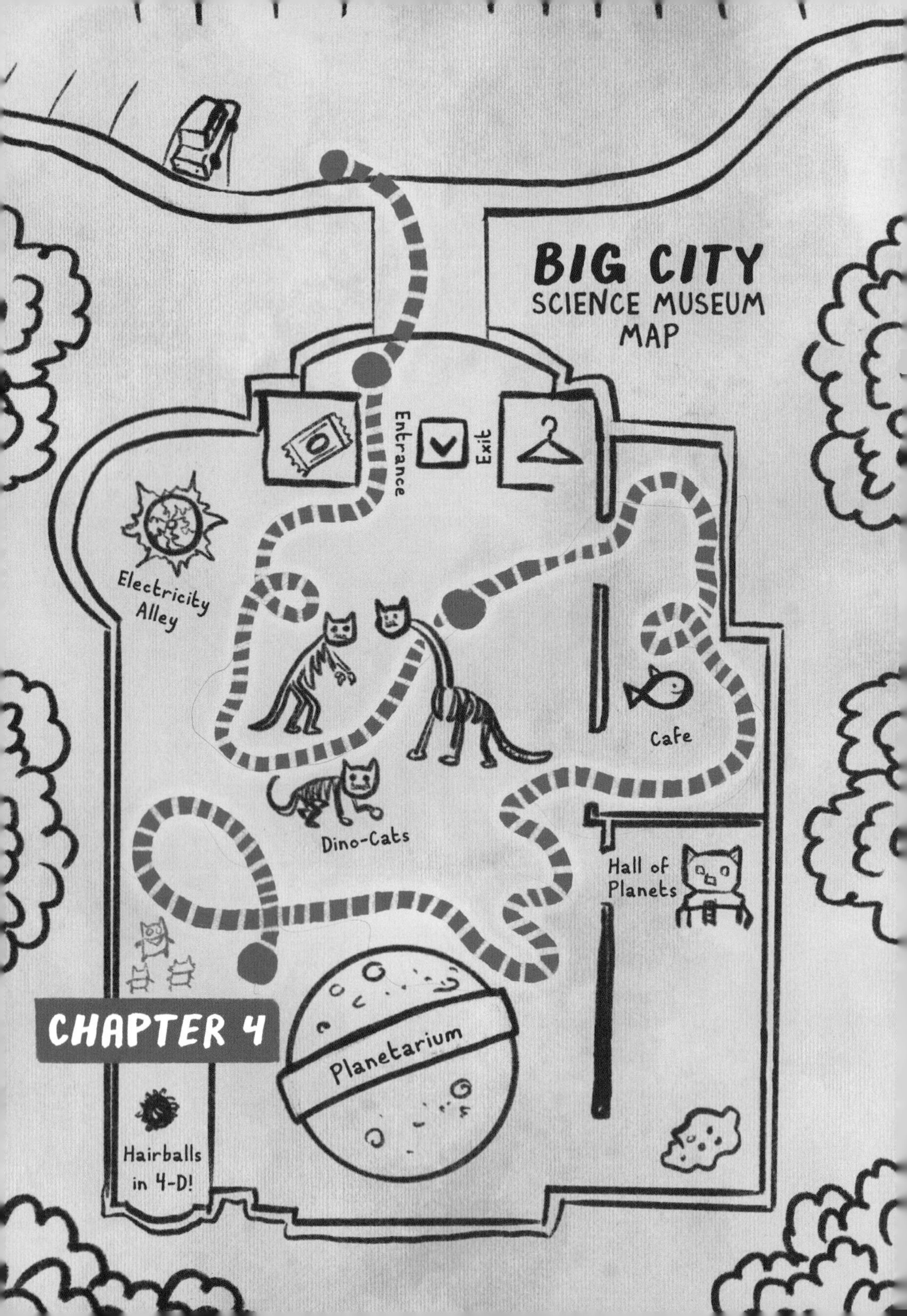
BIG CITY
SCIENCE MUSEUM
MAP
Entrance
Exit
Electricity Alley
Dino-Cats
Cafe
Hall of Planets
Planetarium
Hairballs in 4-D!

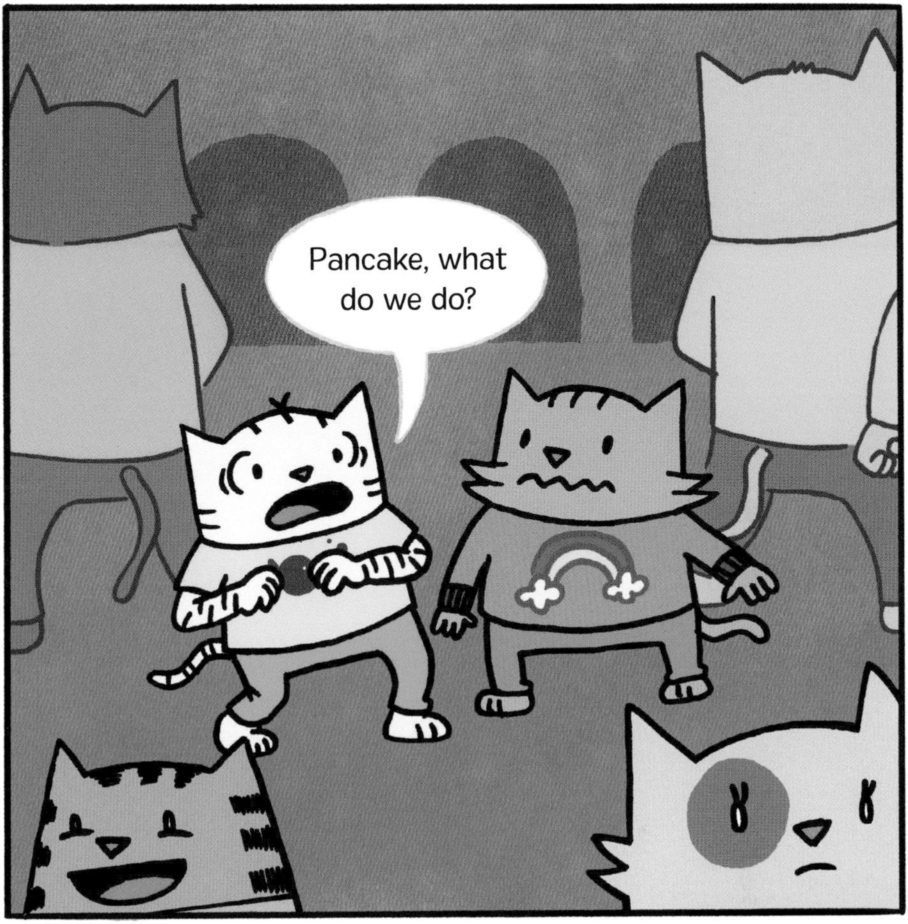
Pancake, what do we do?

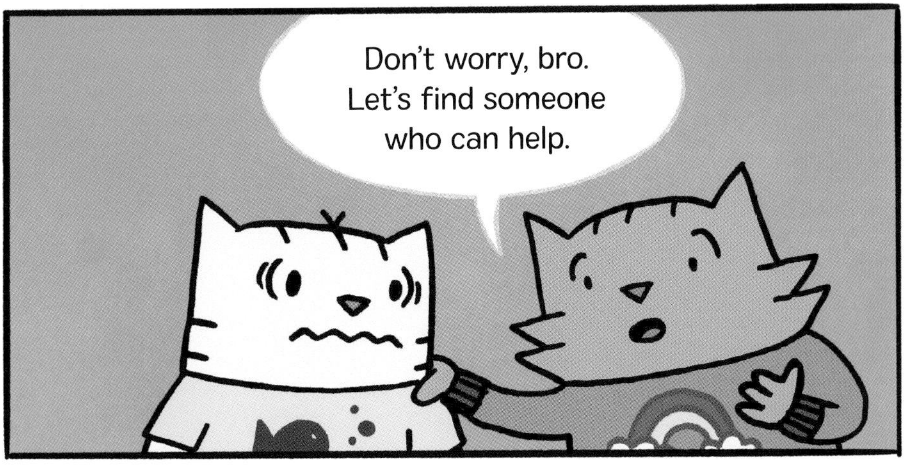
Don't worry, bro. Let's find someone who can help.

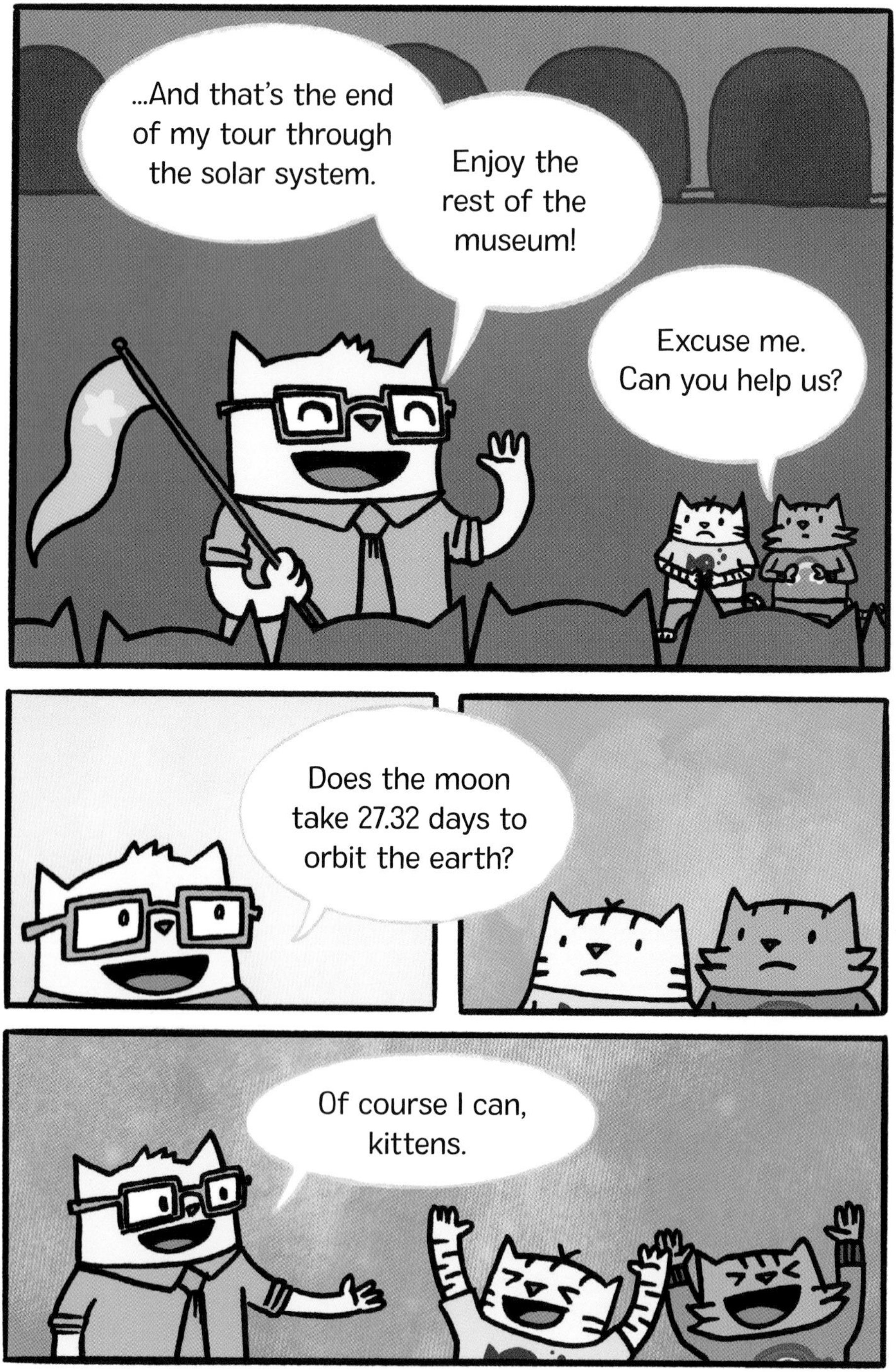
...And that's the end of my tour through the solar system.
Enjoy the rest of the museum!
Excuse me. Can you help us?
Does the moon take 27.32 days to orbit the earth?
Of course I can, kittens.

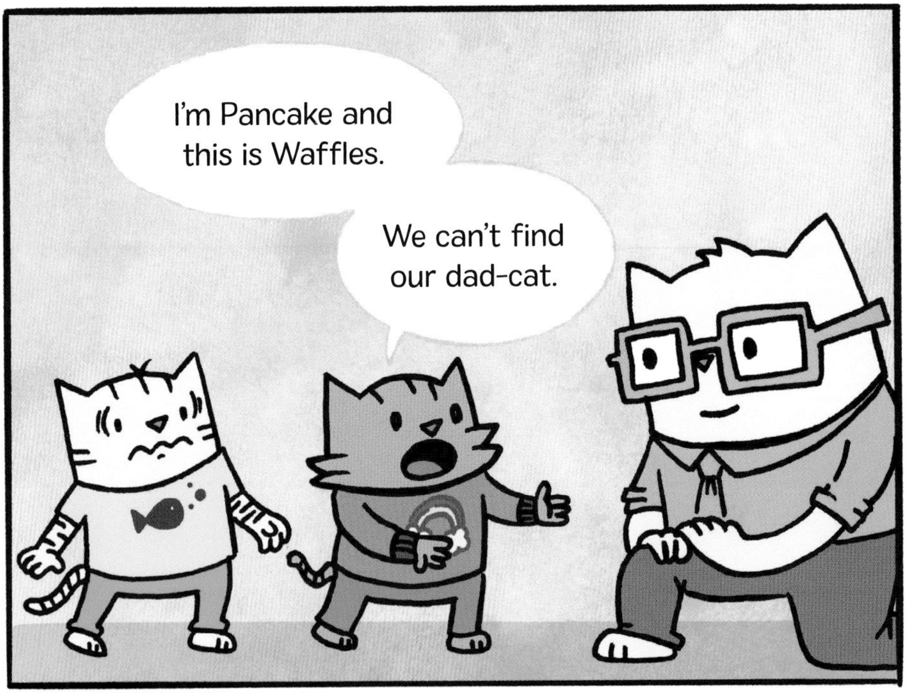
I'm Pancake and this is Waffles.
We can't find our dad-cat.

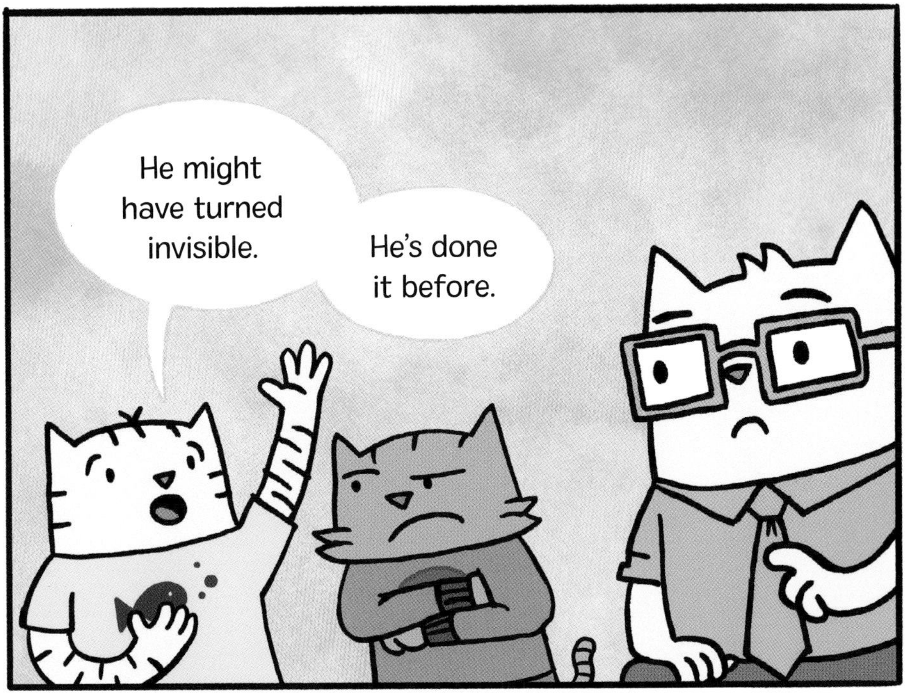
He might have turned invisible.
He's done it before.

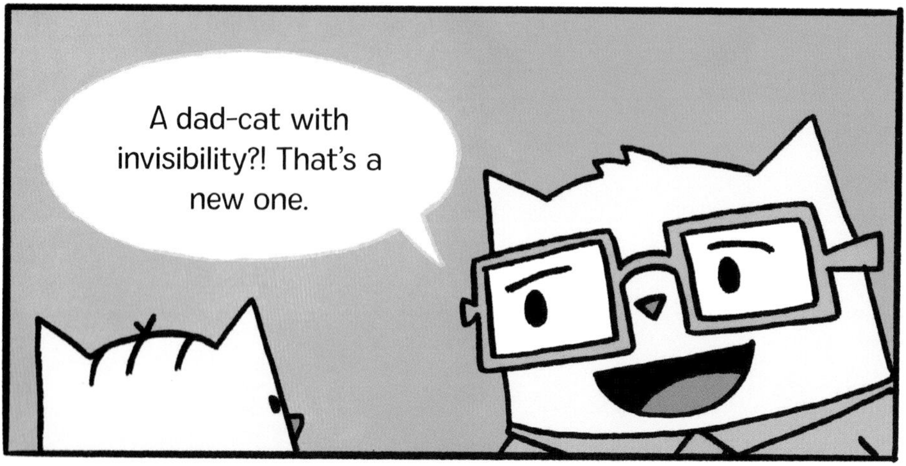
A dad-cat with invisibility?! That's a new one.

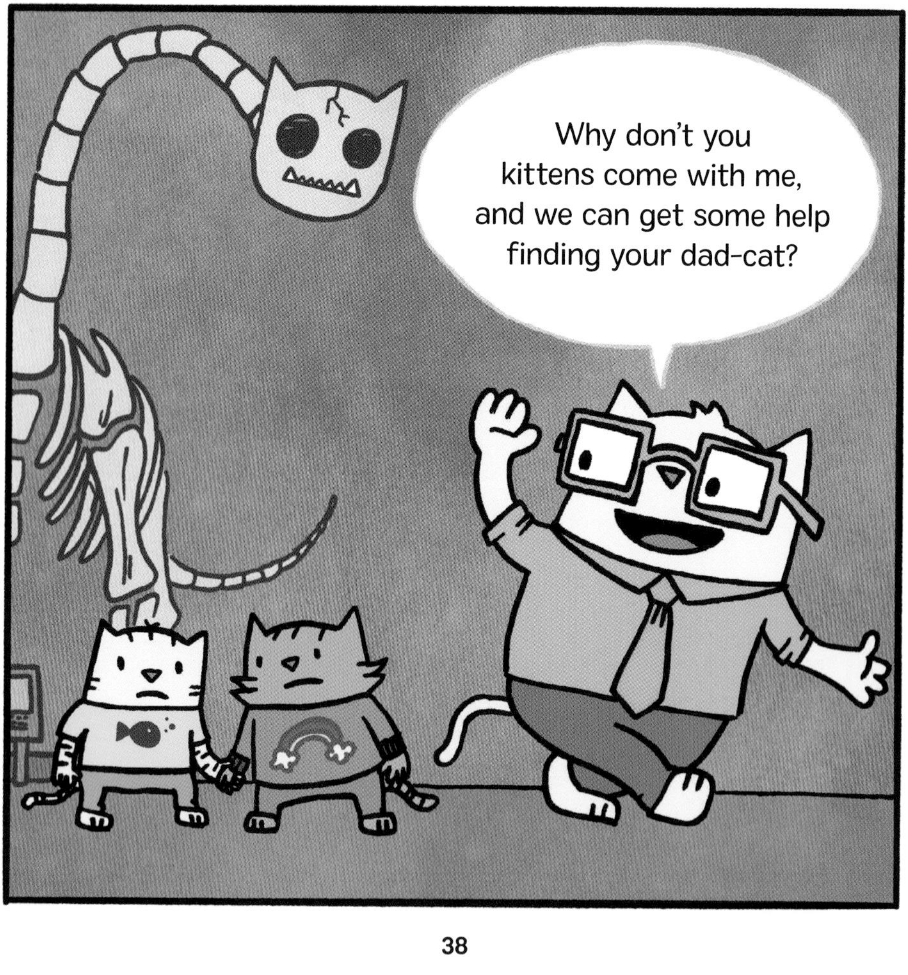
Why don't you kittens come with me, and we can get some help finding your dad-cat?

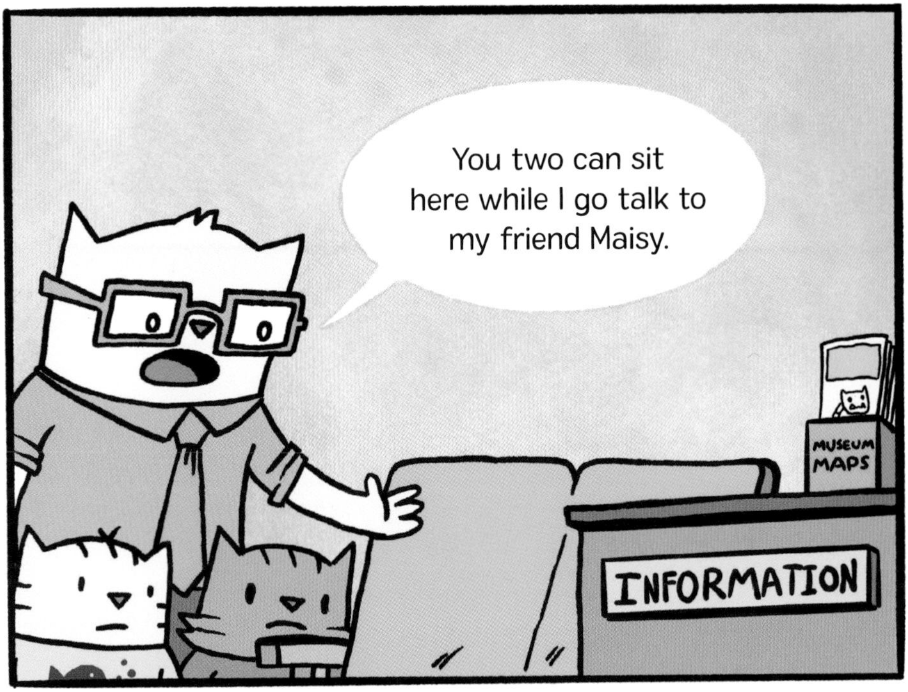
You two can sit here while I go talk to my friend Maisy.
MUSEUM MAPS
INFORMATION

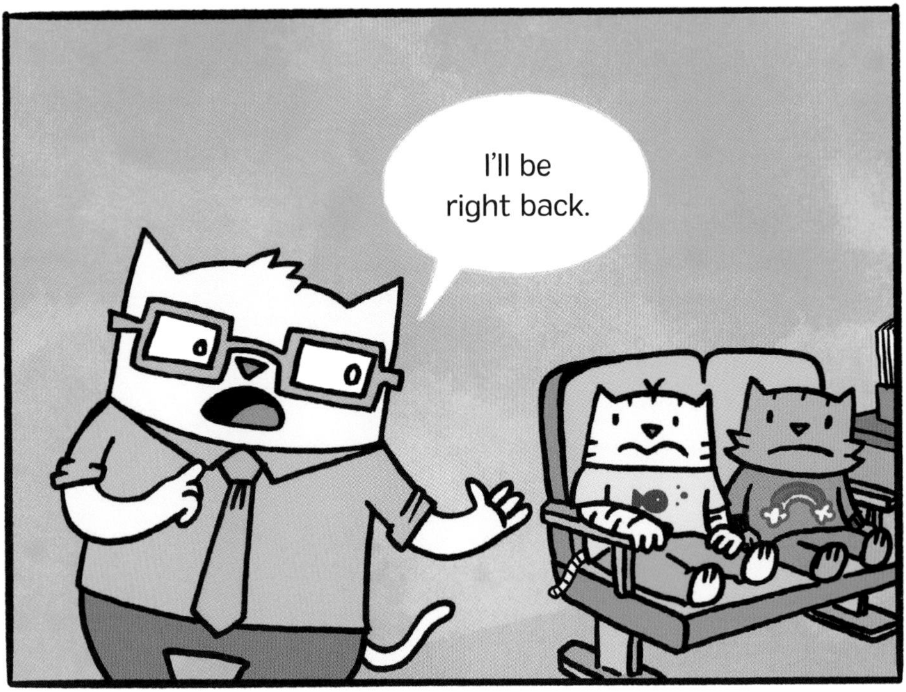
I'll be right back.

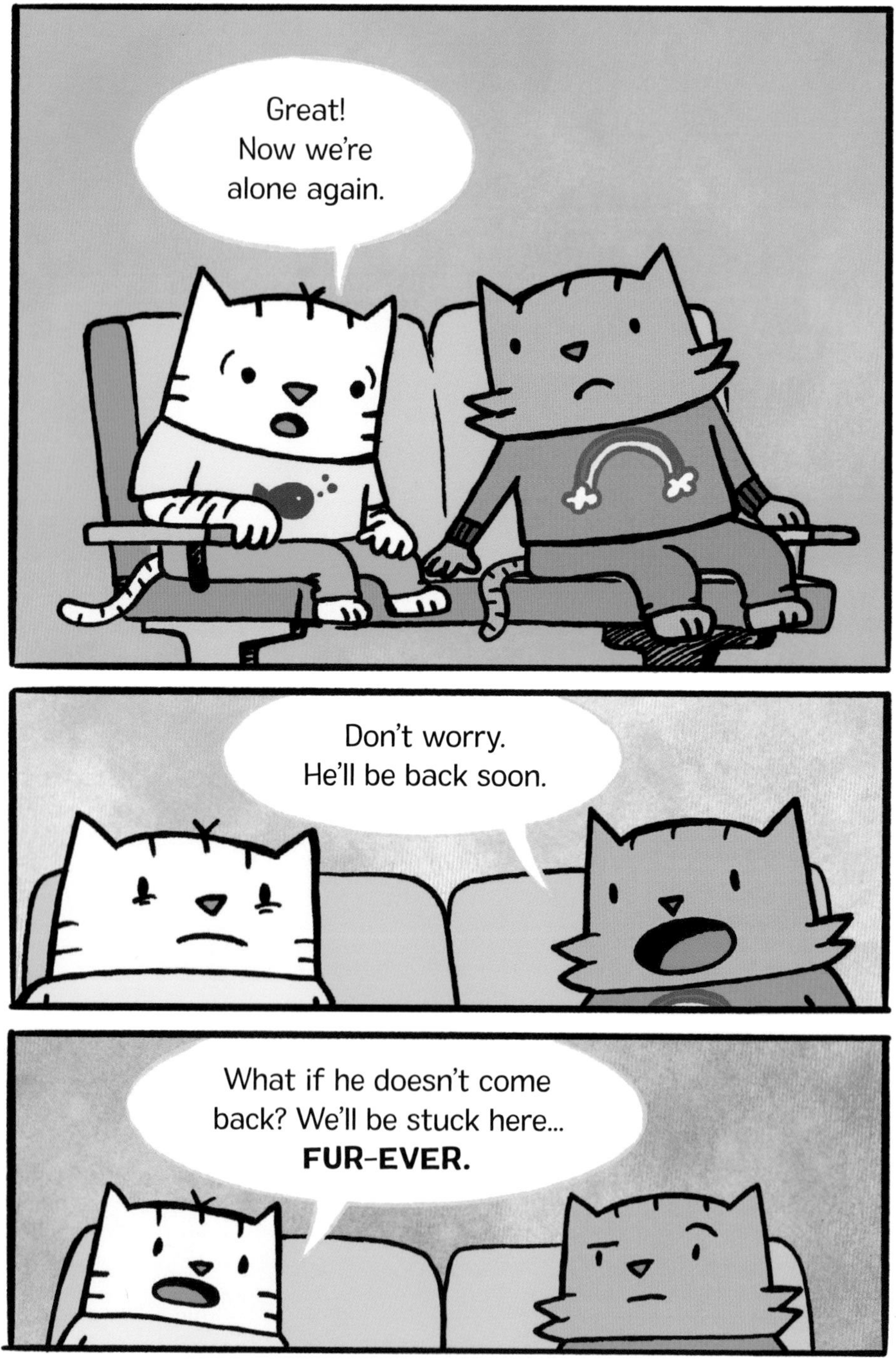
Great!
Now we're
alone again.
Don't worry.
He'll be back soon.
What if he doesn't come
back? We'll be stuck here...
FUR-EVER.

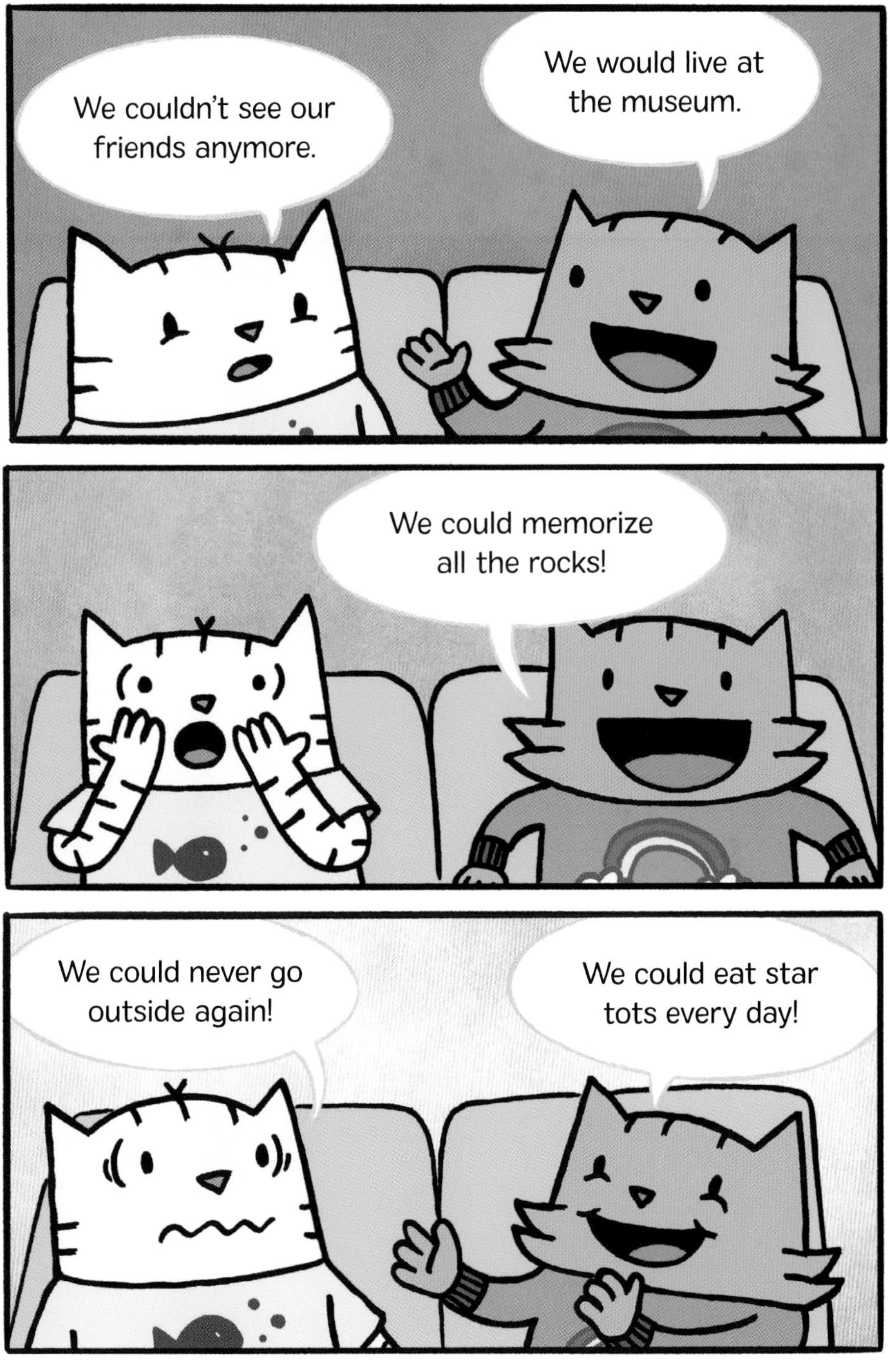
We couldn't see our friends anymore.
We would live at the museum.
We could memorize all the rocks!
We could never go outside again!
We could eat star tots every day!

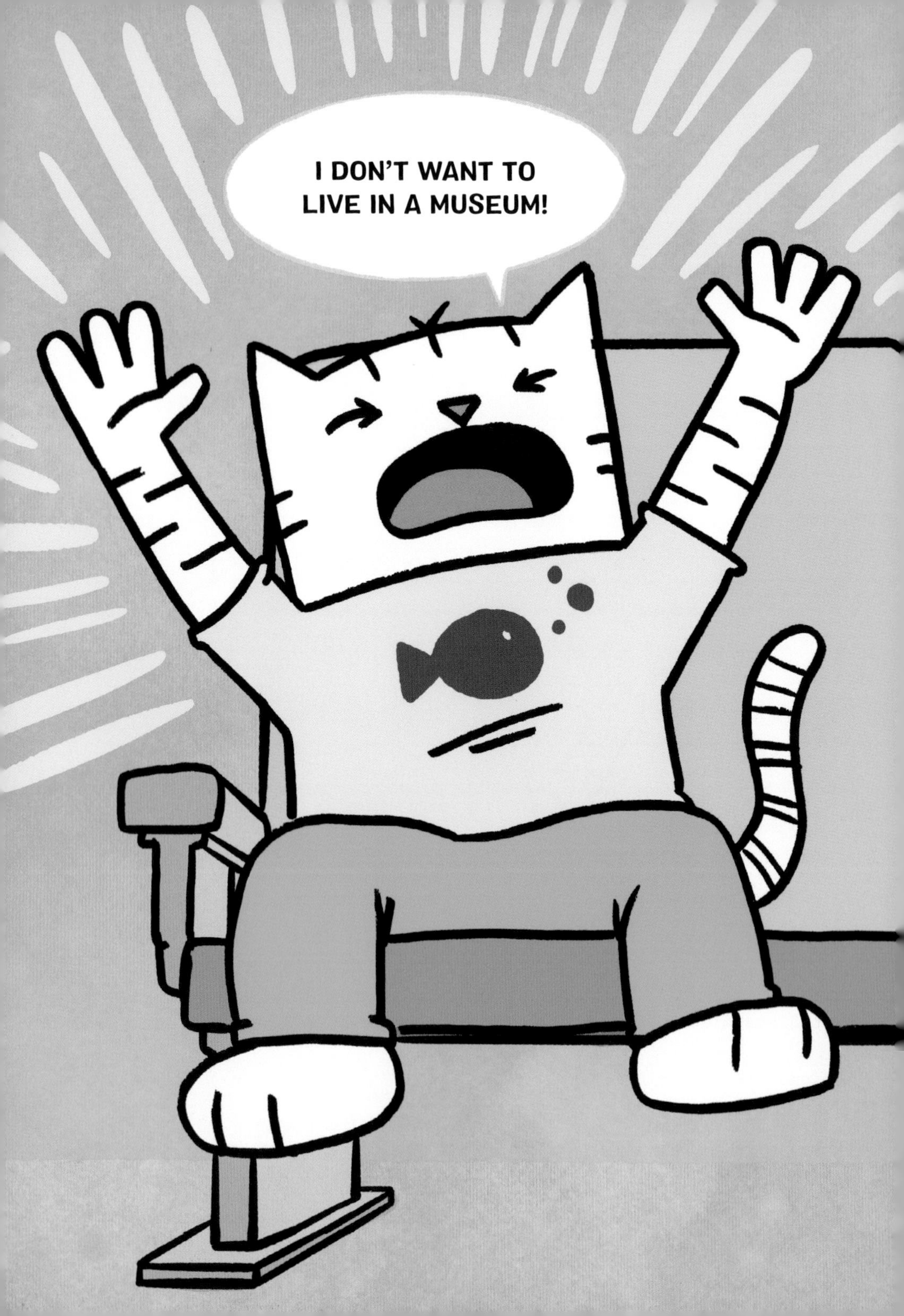
I DON'T WANT TO LIVE IN A MUSEUM!

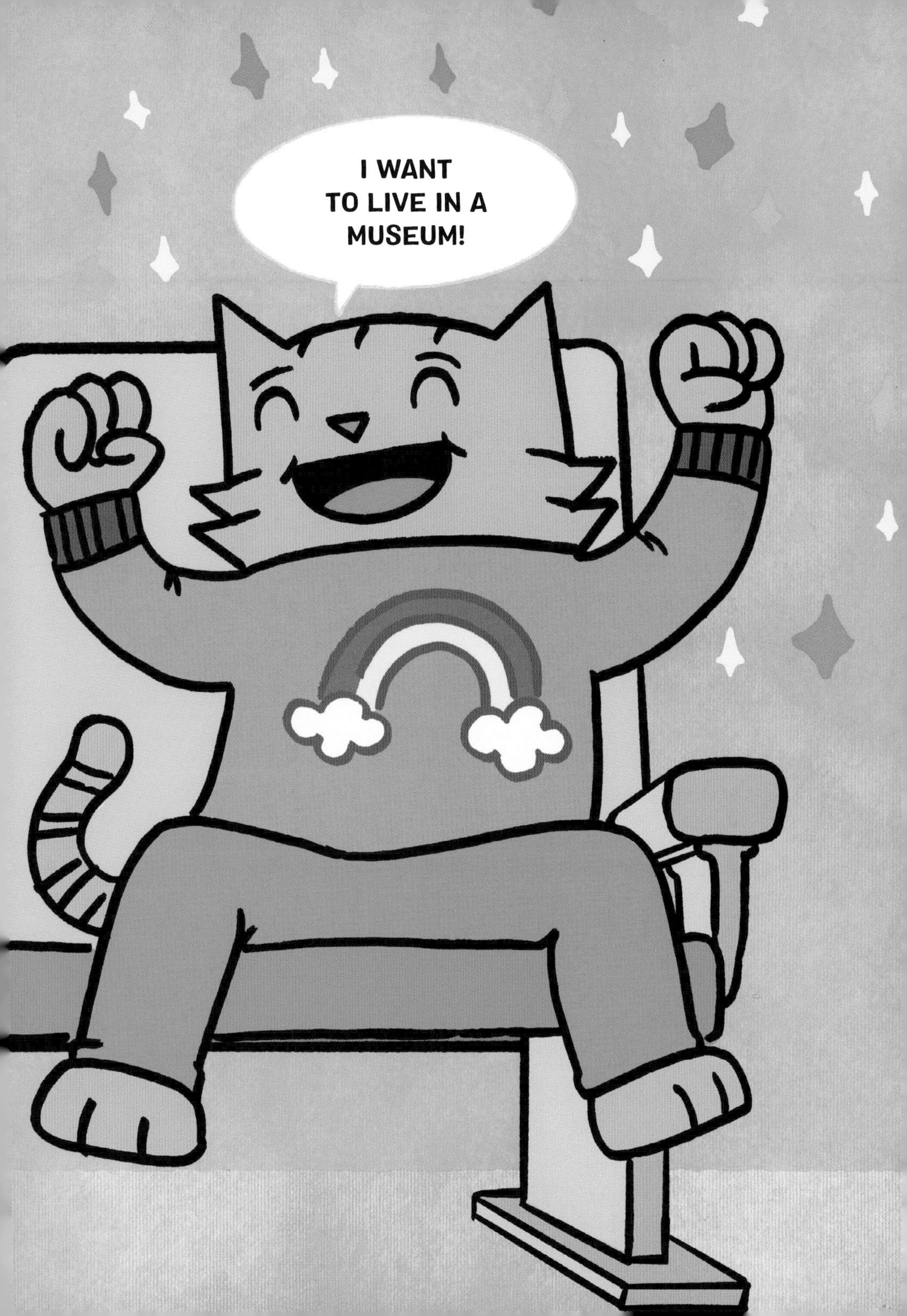
I WANT TO LIVE IN A MUSEUM!

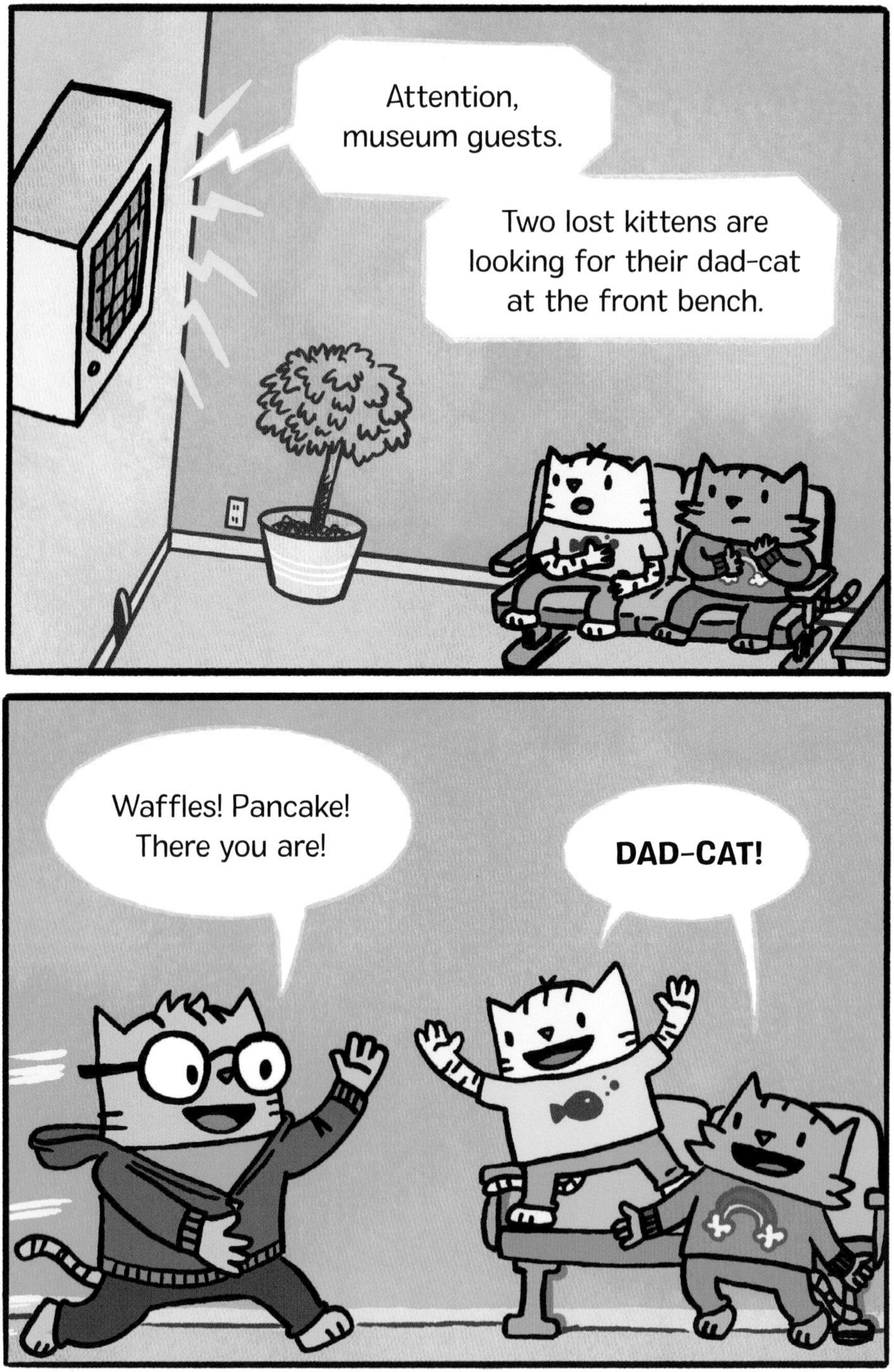
Attention, museum guests.
Two lost kittens are looking for their dad-cat at the front bench.
Waffles! Pancake! There you are!
DAD-CAT!

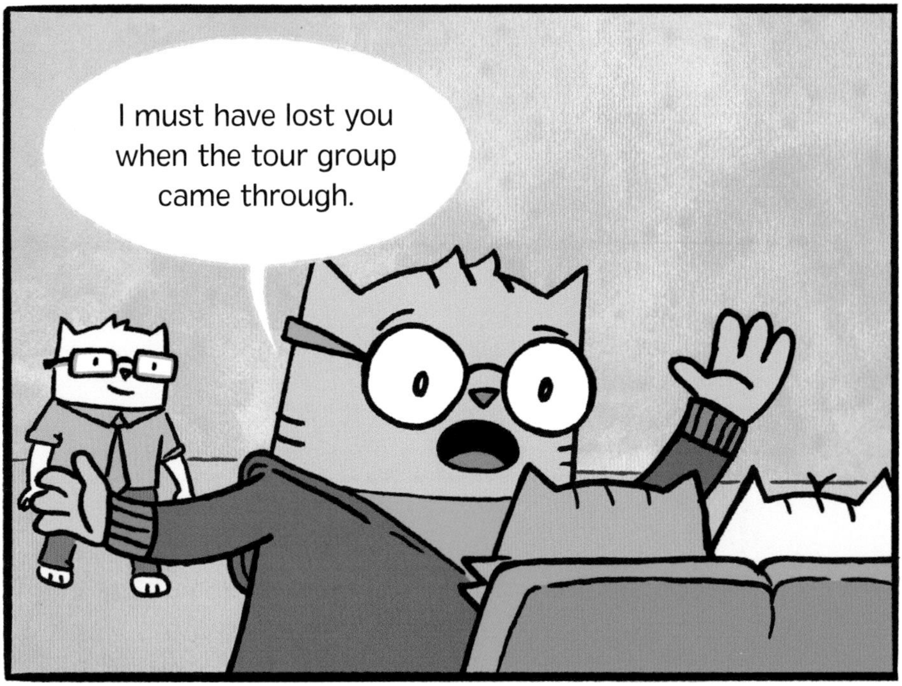
I must have lost you when the tour group came through.

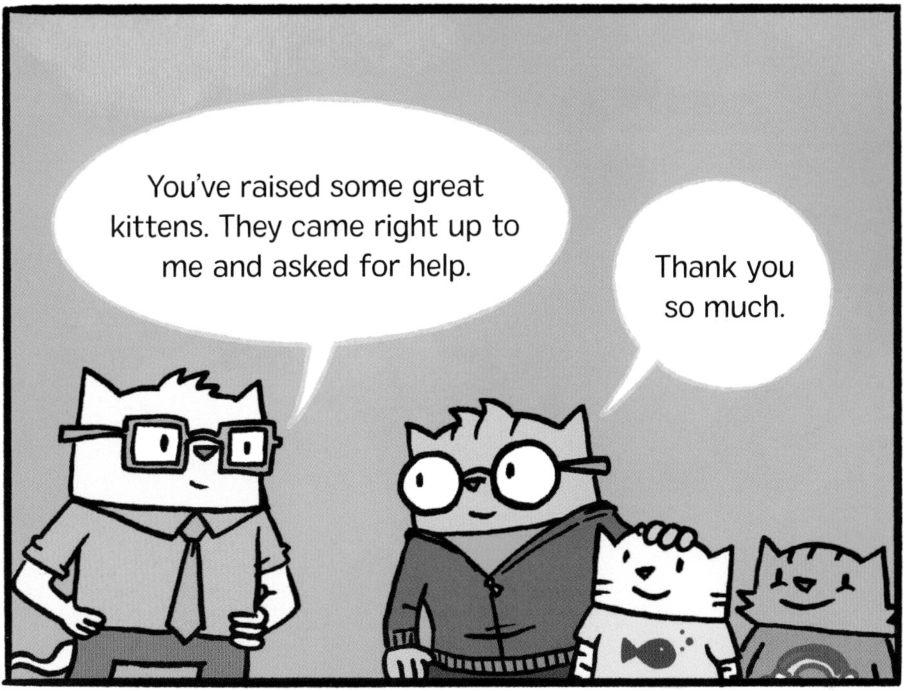
You've raised some great kittens. They came right up to me and asked for help.
Thank you so much.

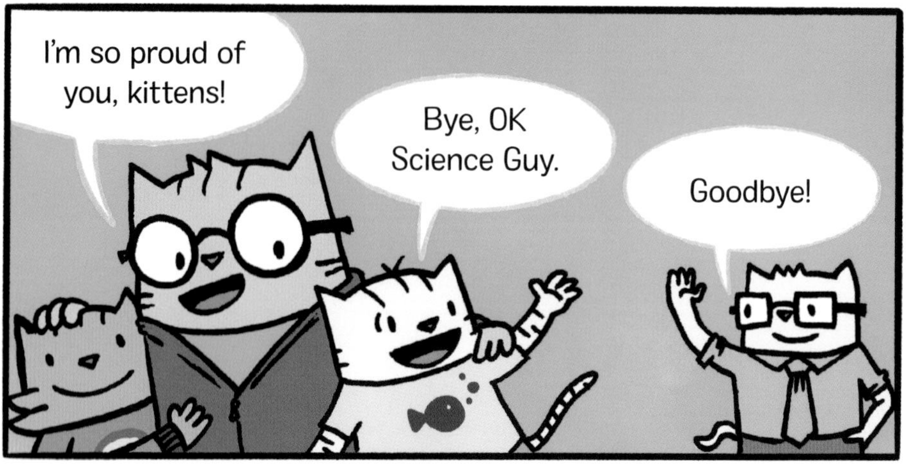
I'm so proud of you, kittens!
Bye, OK Science Guy.
Goodbye!

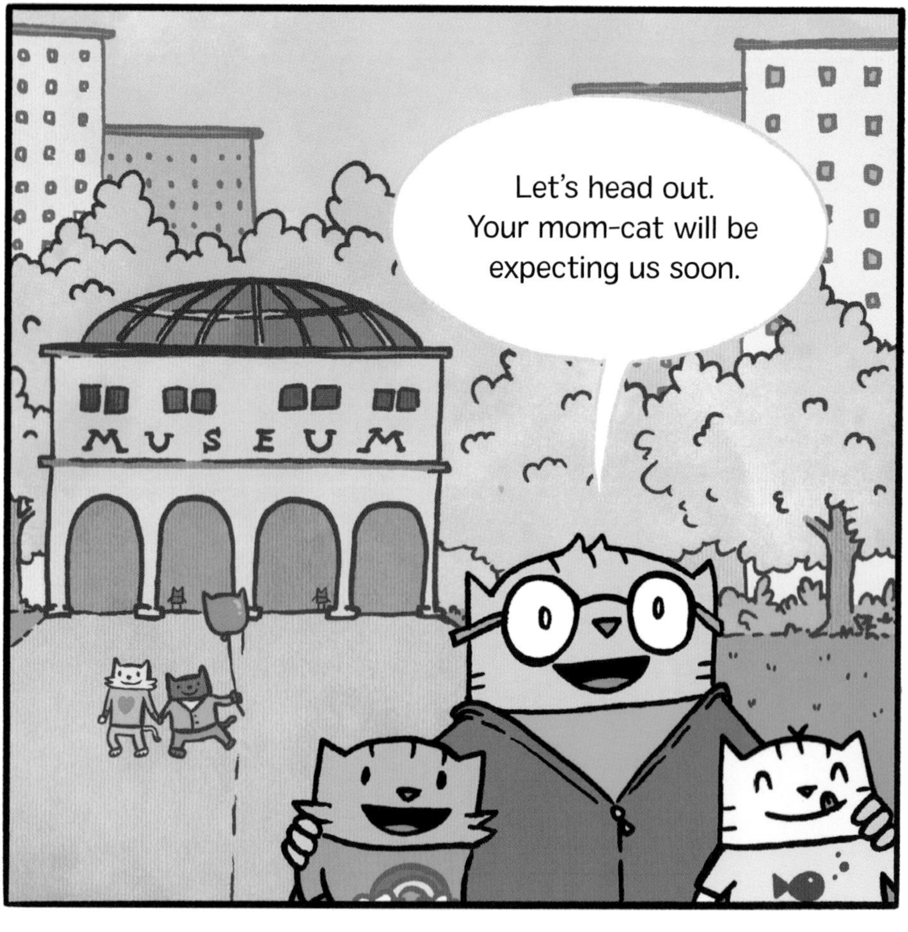
Let's head out. Your mom-cat will be expecting us soon.
MUSEUM

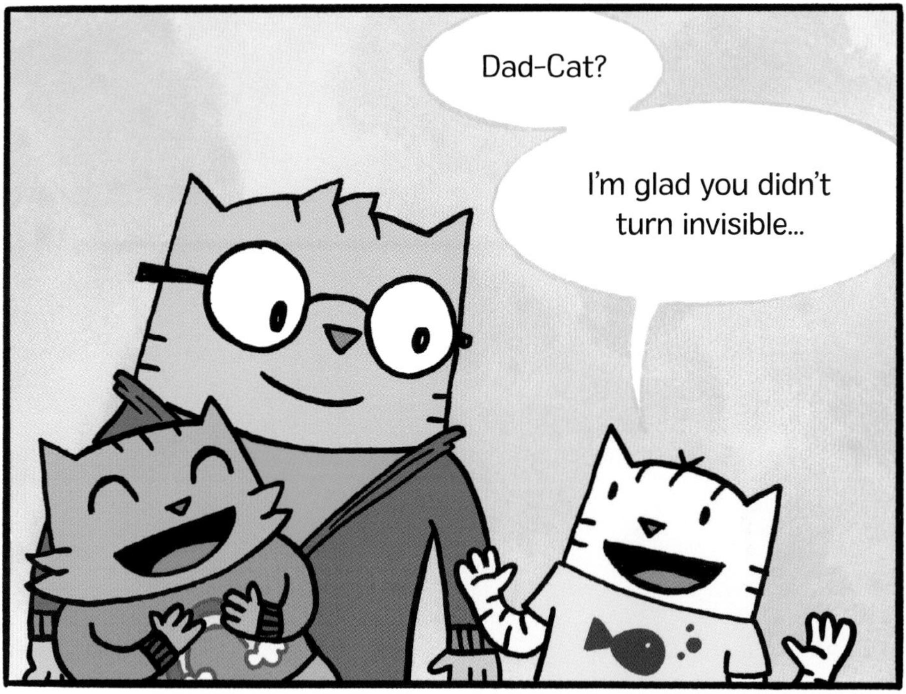
Dad-Cat?
I'm glad you didn't turn invisible...

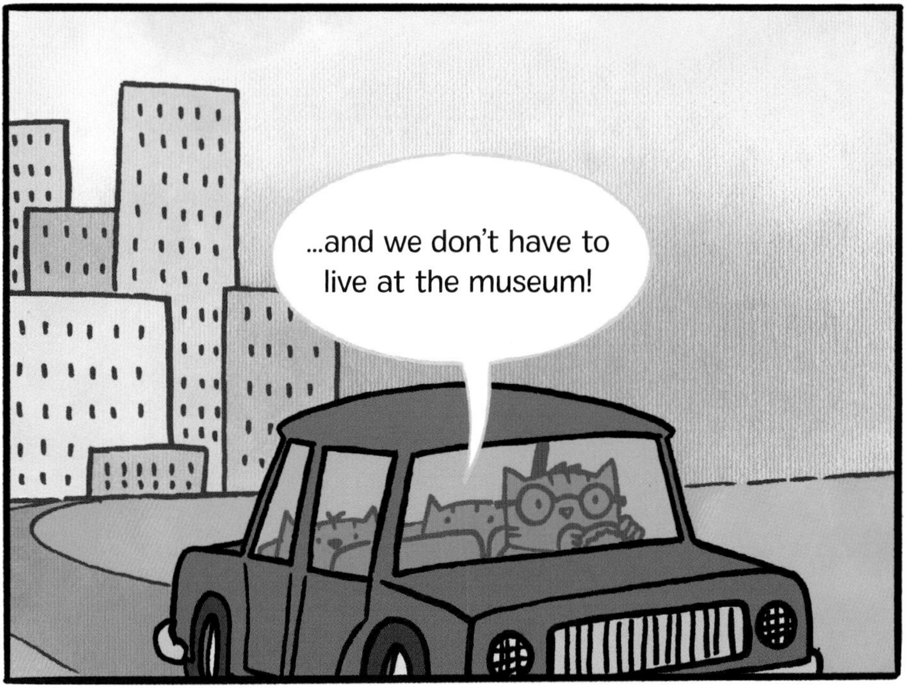
...and we don't have to live at the museum!

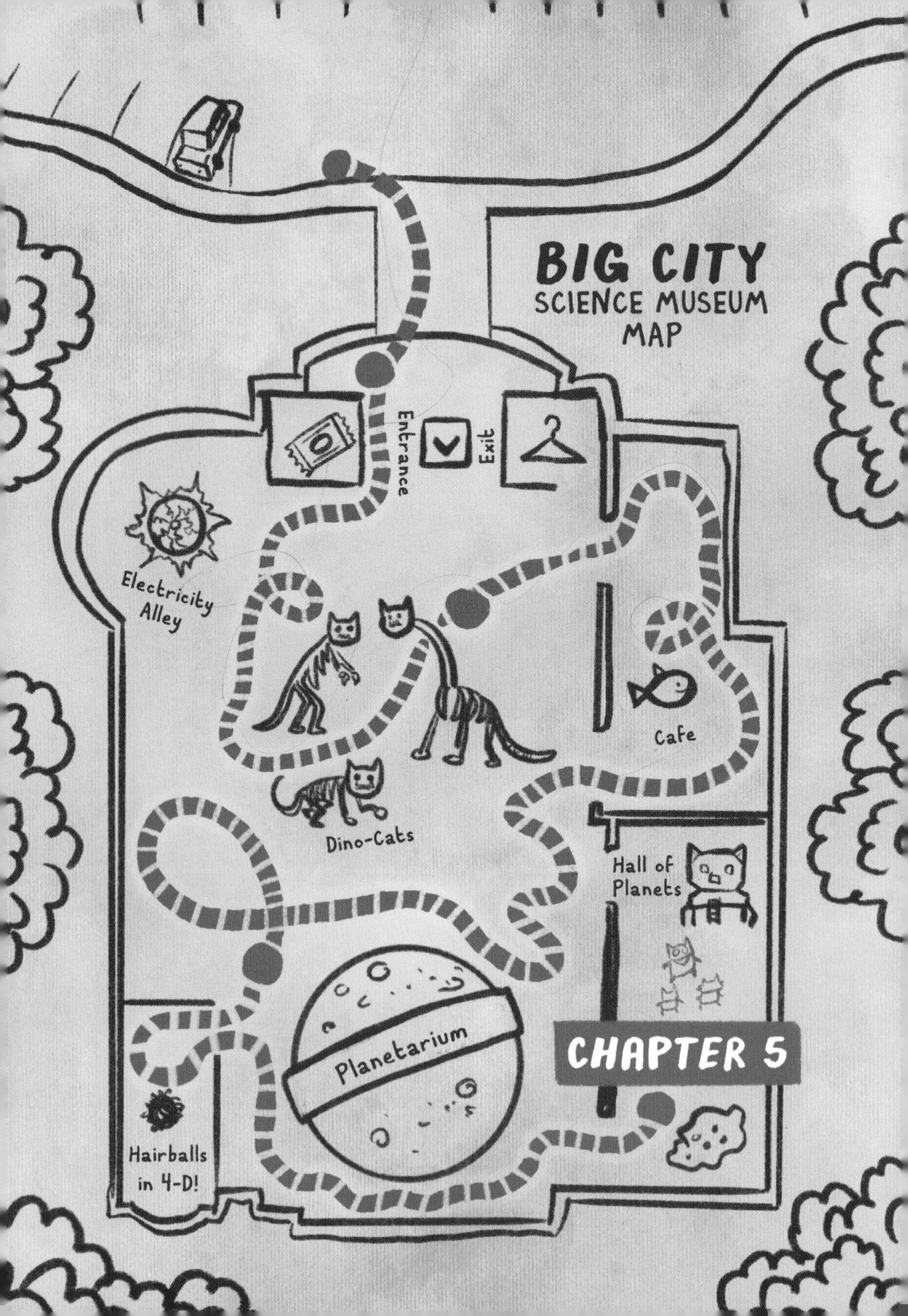
BIG CITY
SCIENCE MUSEUM
MAP
Entrance
Exit
Electricity Alley
Cafe
Dino-Cats
Hall of Planets
Planetarium
Hairballs in 4-D!

CHAPTER 5

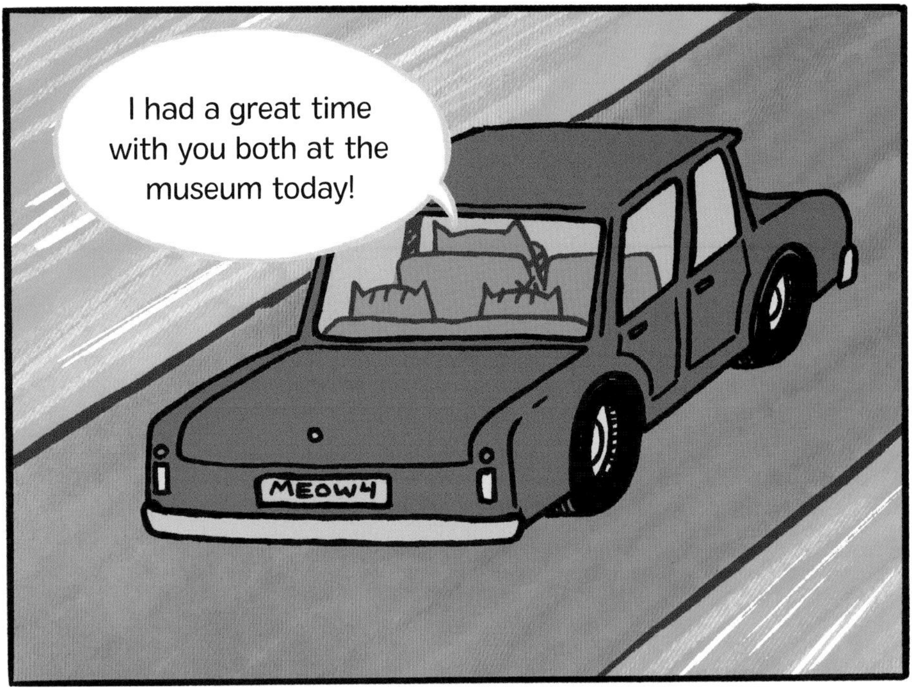
I had a great time with you both at the museum today!
MEOW4

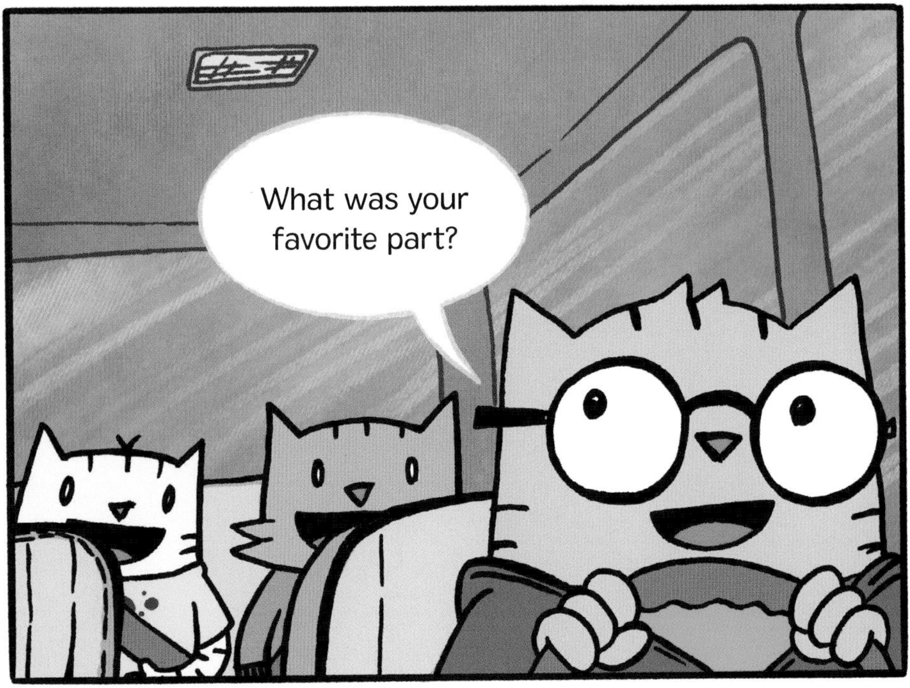
What was your favorite part?

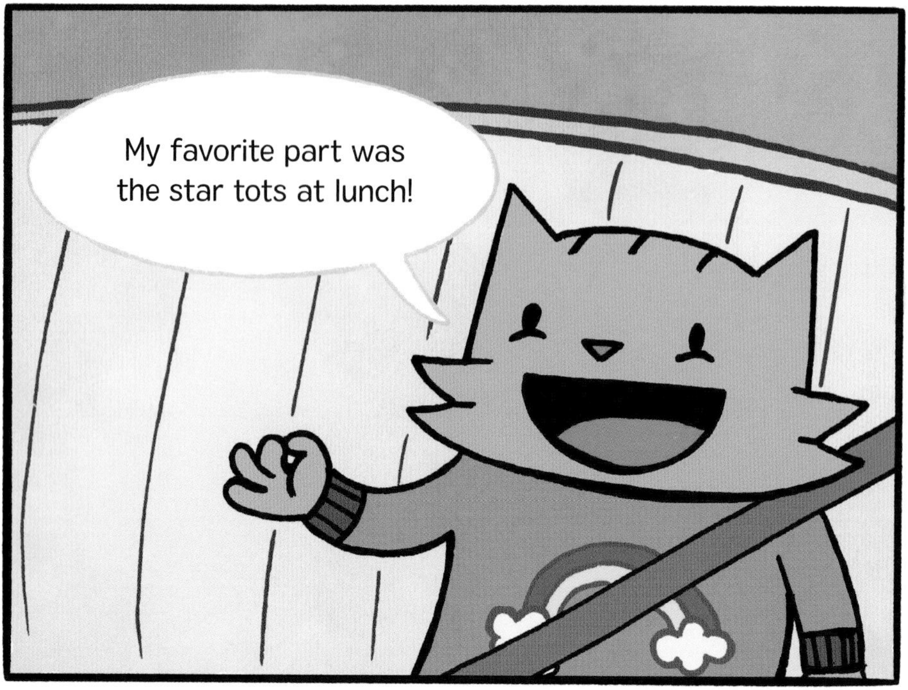
My favorite part was the star tots at lunch!

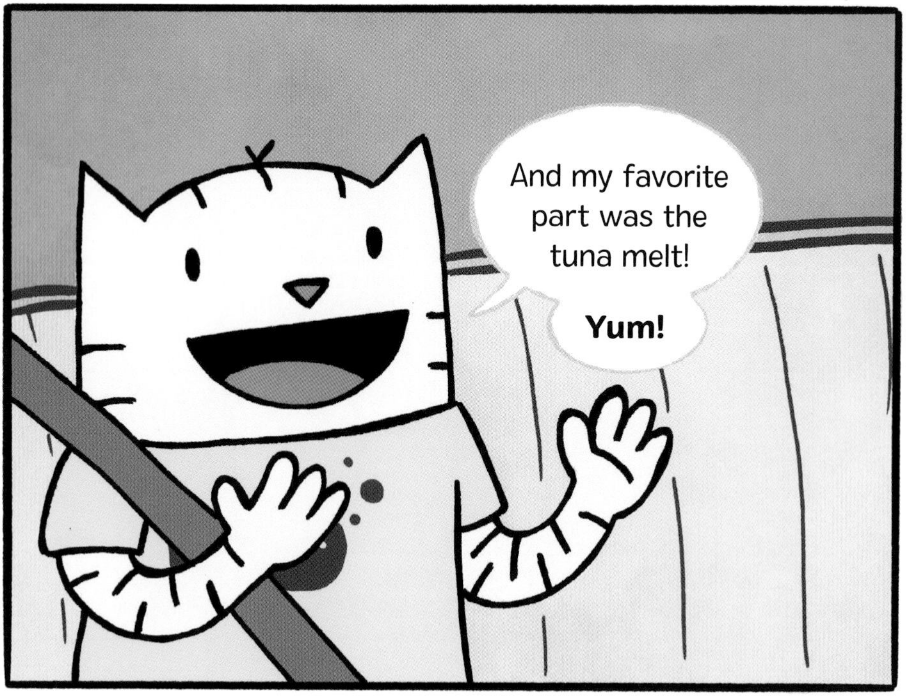
And my favorite part was the tuna melt!
Yum!

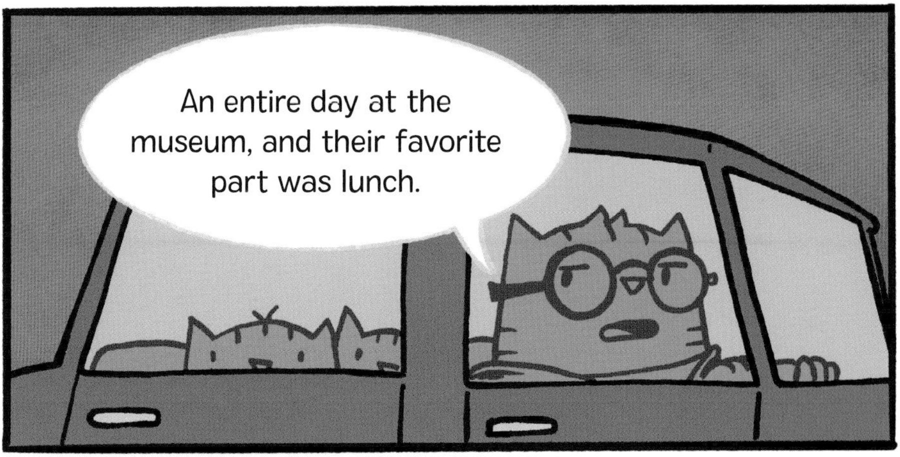
An entire day at the museum, and their favorite part was lunch.

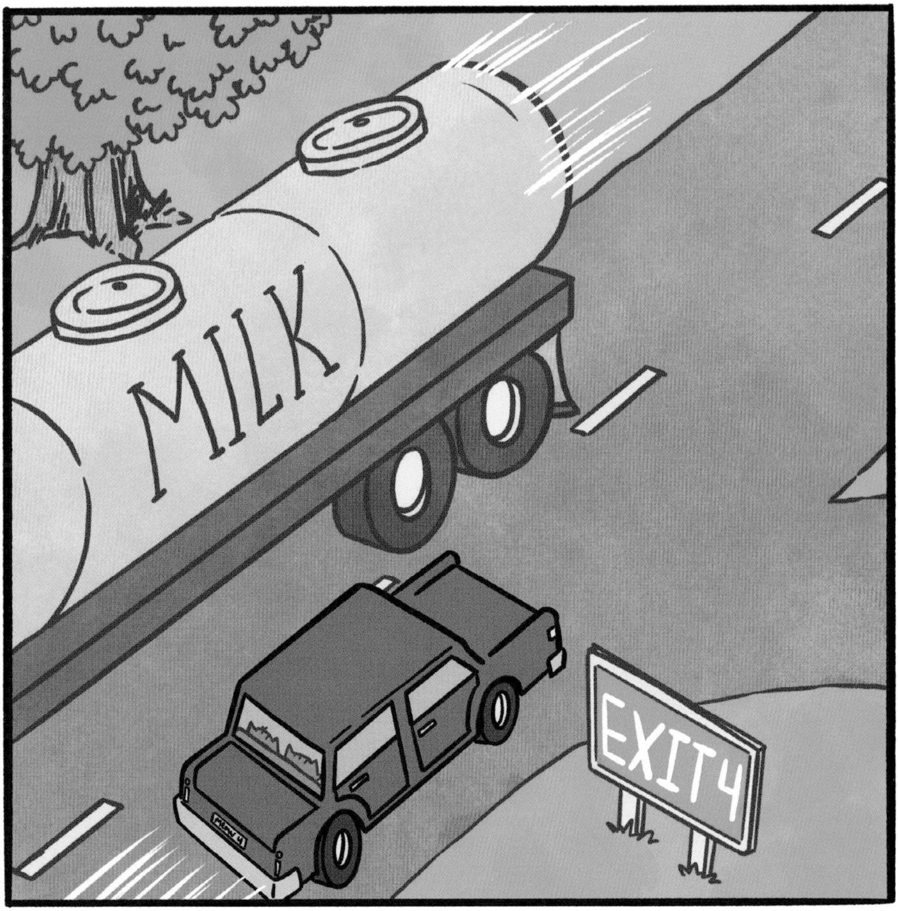
MILK
EXIT 4

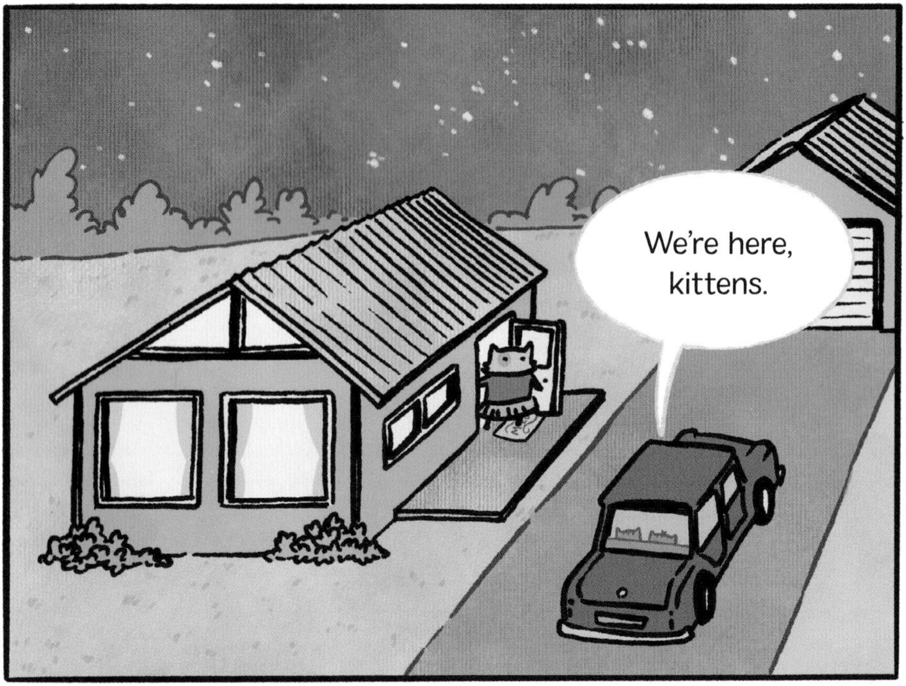
We're here, kittens.

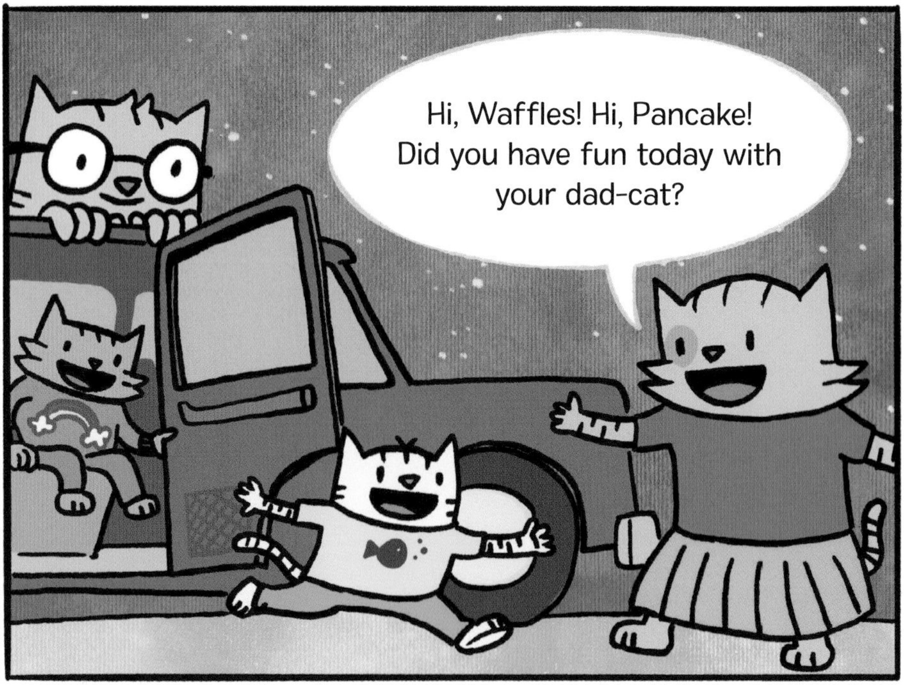
Hi, Waffles! Hi, Pancake! Did you have fun today with your dad-cat?

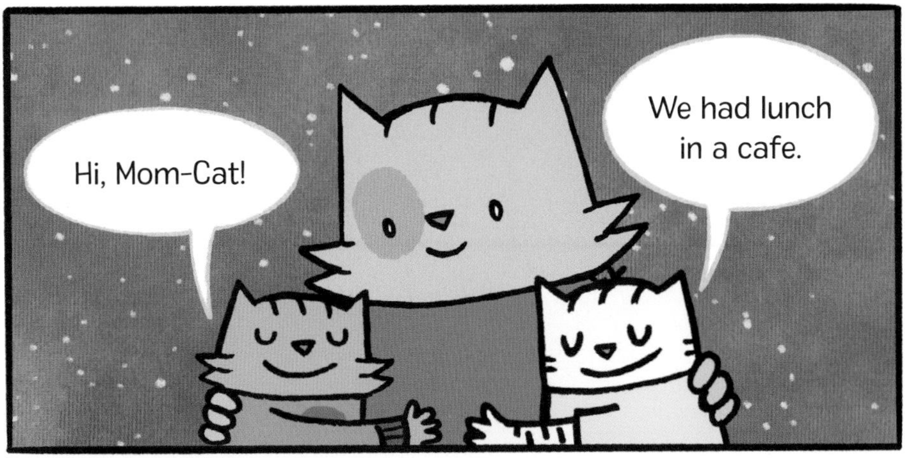
Hi, Mom-Cat!
We had lunch in a cafe.

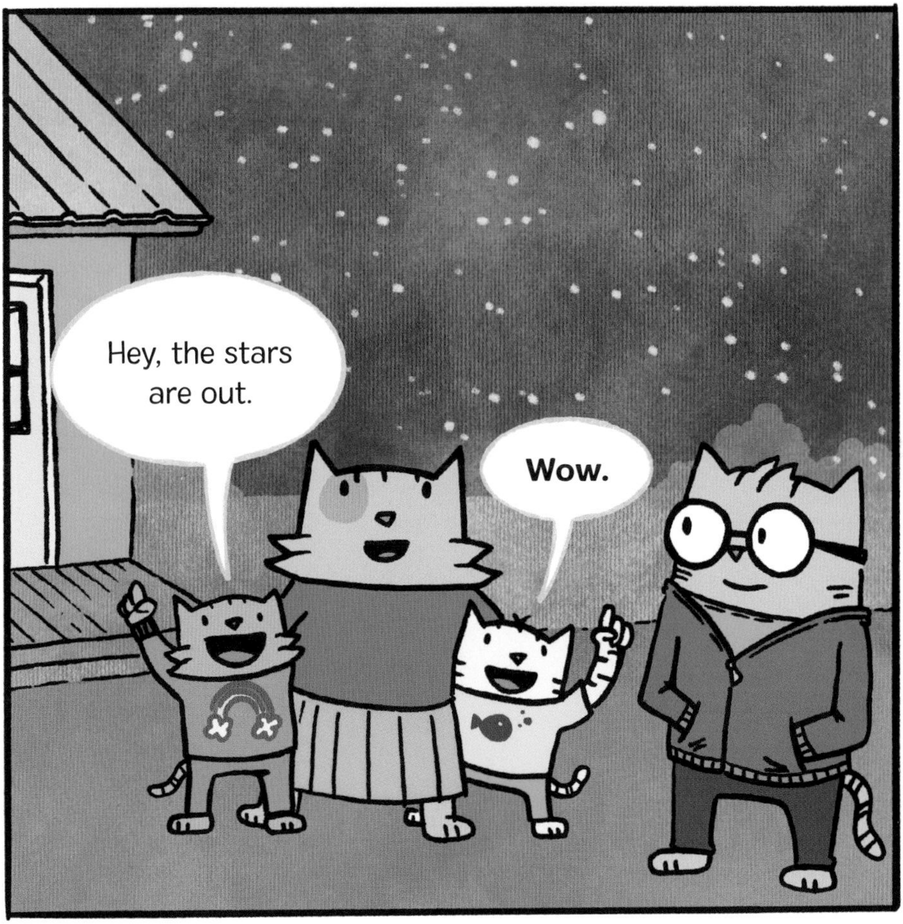
Hey, the stars are out.
Wow.

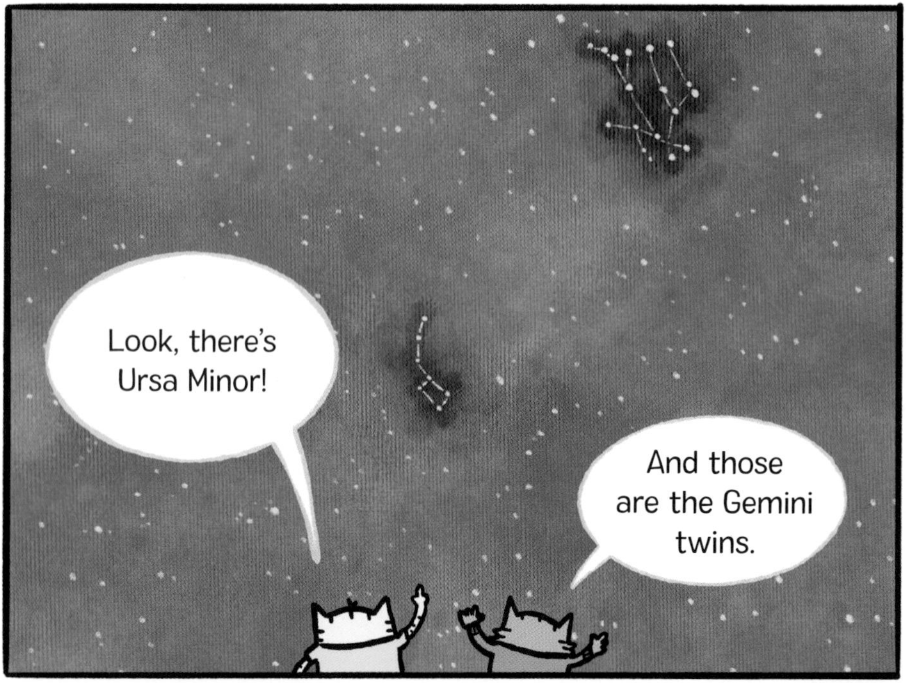
Look, there's Ursa Minor!
And those are the Gemini twins.

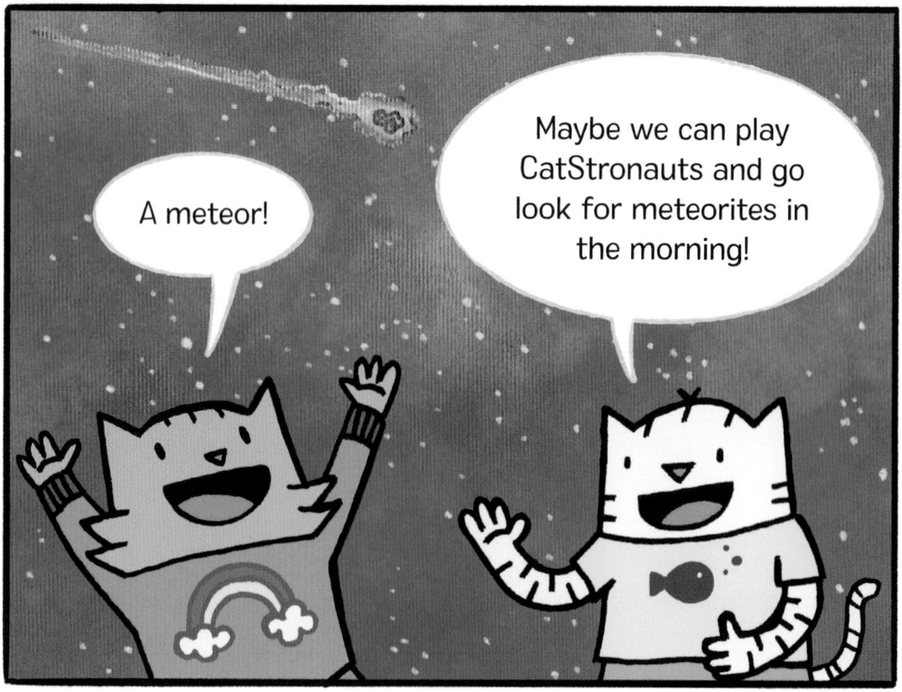
A meteor!
Maybe we can play CatStronauts and go look for meteorites in the morning!

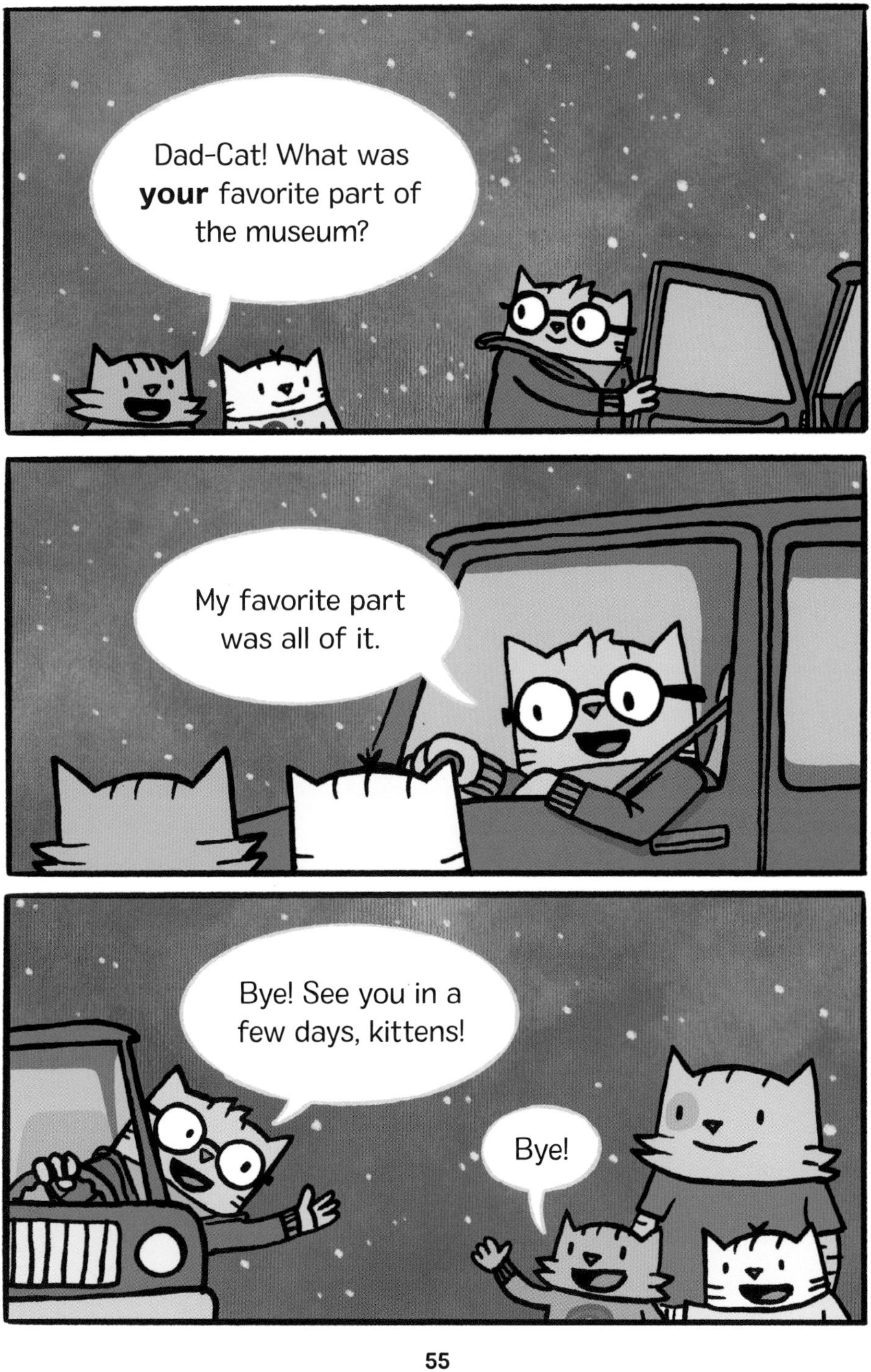
Dad-Cat! What was **your** favorite part of the museum?
My favorite part was all of it.
Bye! See you in a few days, kittens!
Bye!

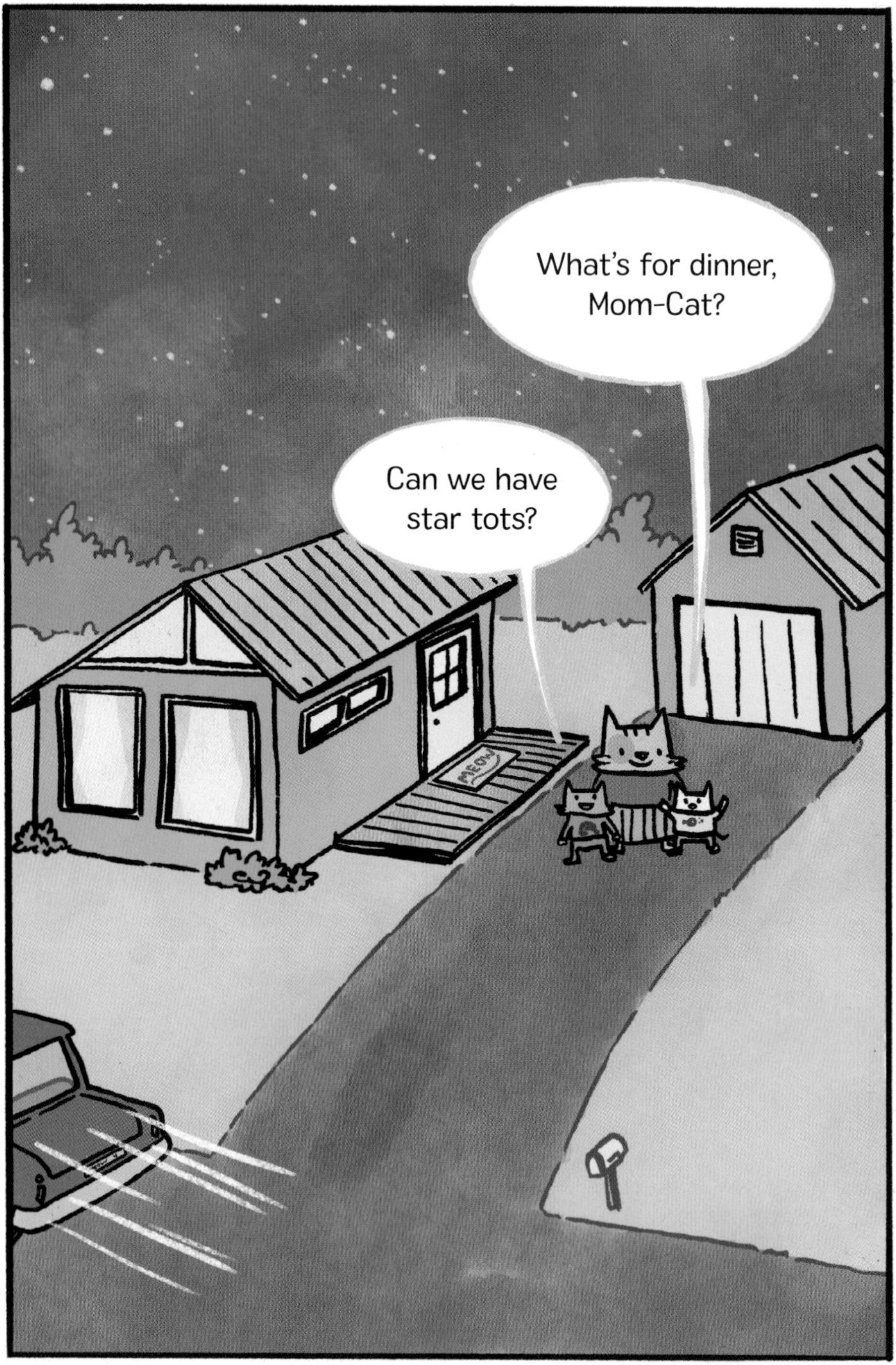
What's for dinner, Mom-Cat?
Can we have star tots?
MEOW

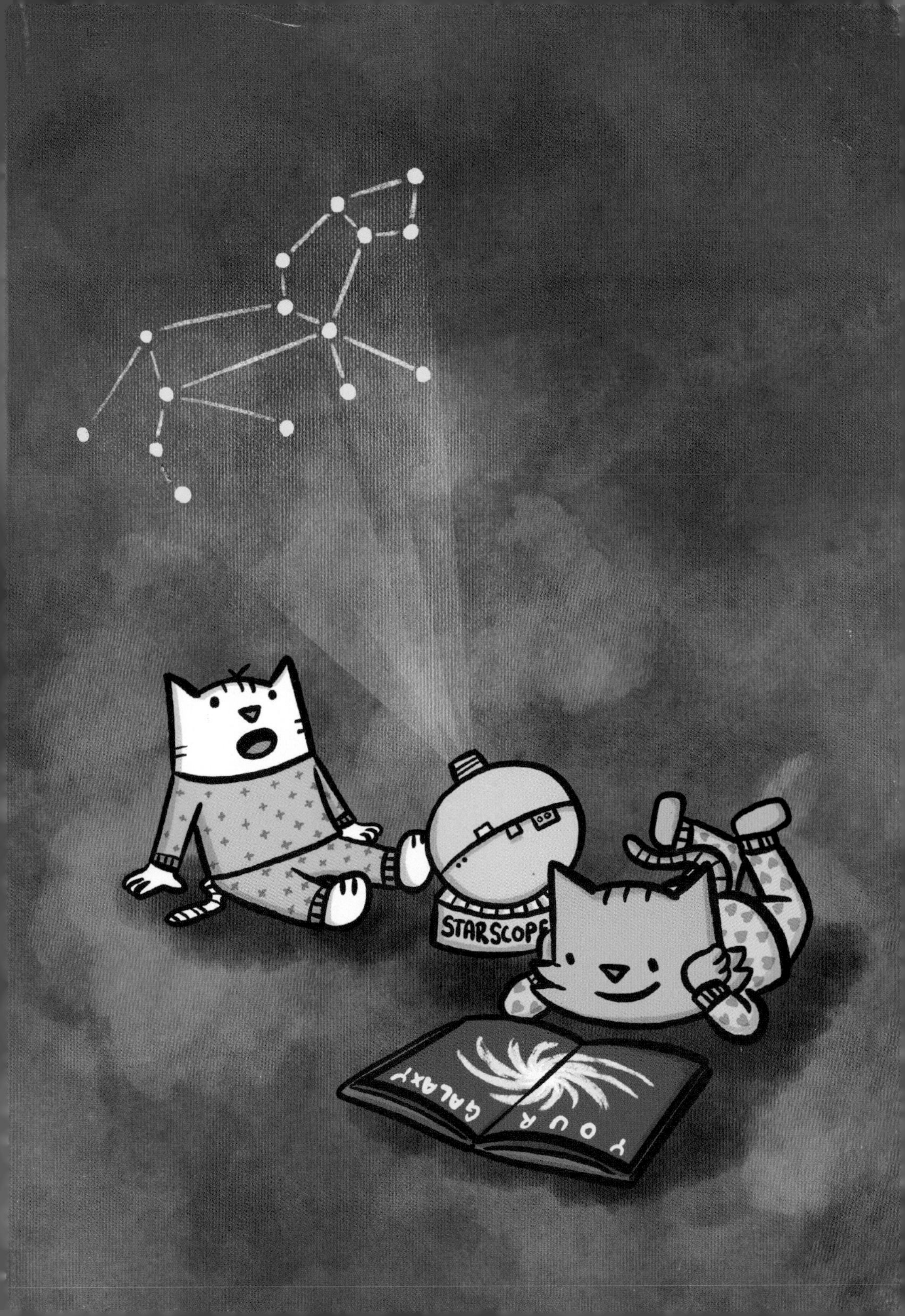
STARSCOPE
YOUR GALAXY

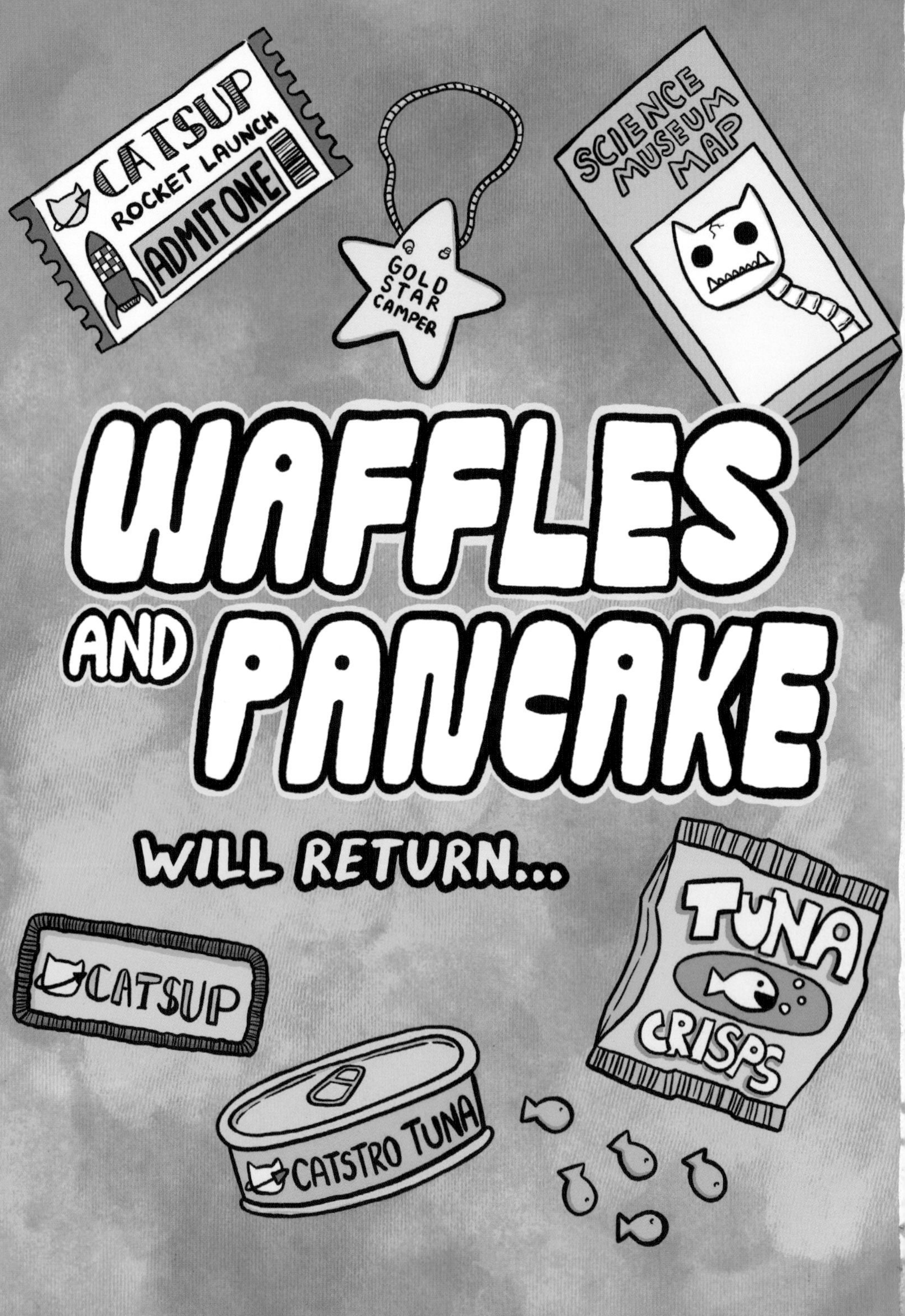

CATSUP
ROCKET LAUNCH
ADMIT ONE
GOLD STAR CAMPER
SCIENCE MUSEUM MAP
WAFFLES
AND PANCAKE
WILL RETURN...
CATSUP
TUNA CRISPS
CATSTRO TUNA

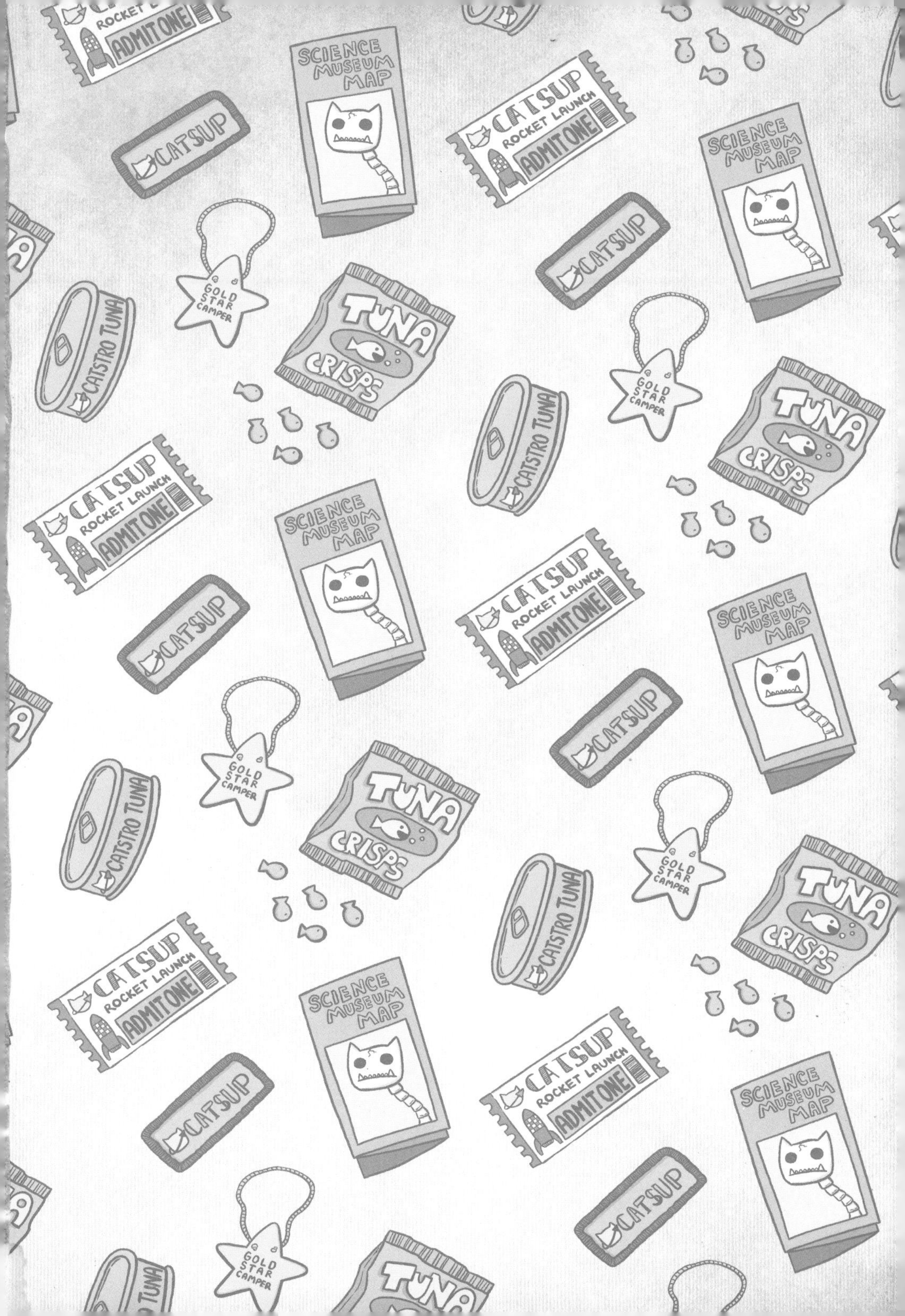
CATSUP
ROCKET LAUNCH
ADMIT ONE
SCIENCE MUSEUM MAP
CATSUP
GOLD STAR CAMPER
CATSTRO TUNA
TUNA CRISPS

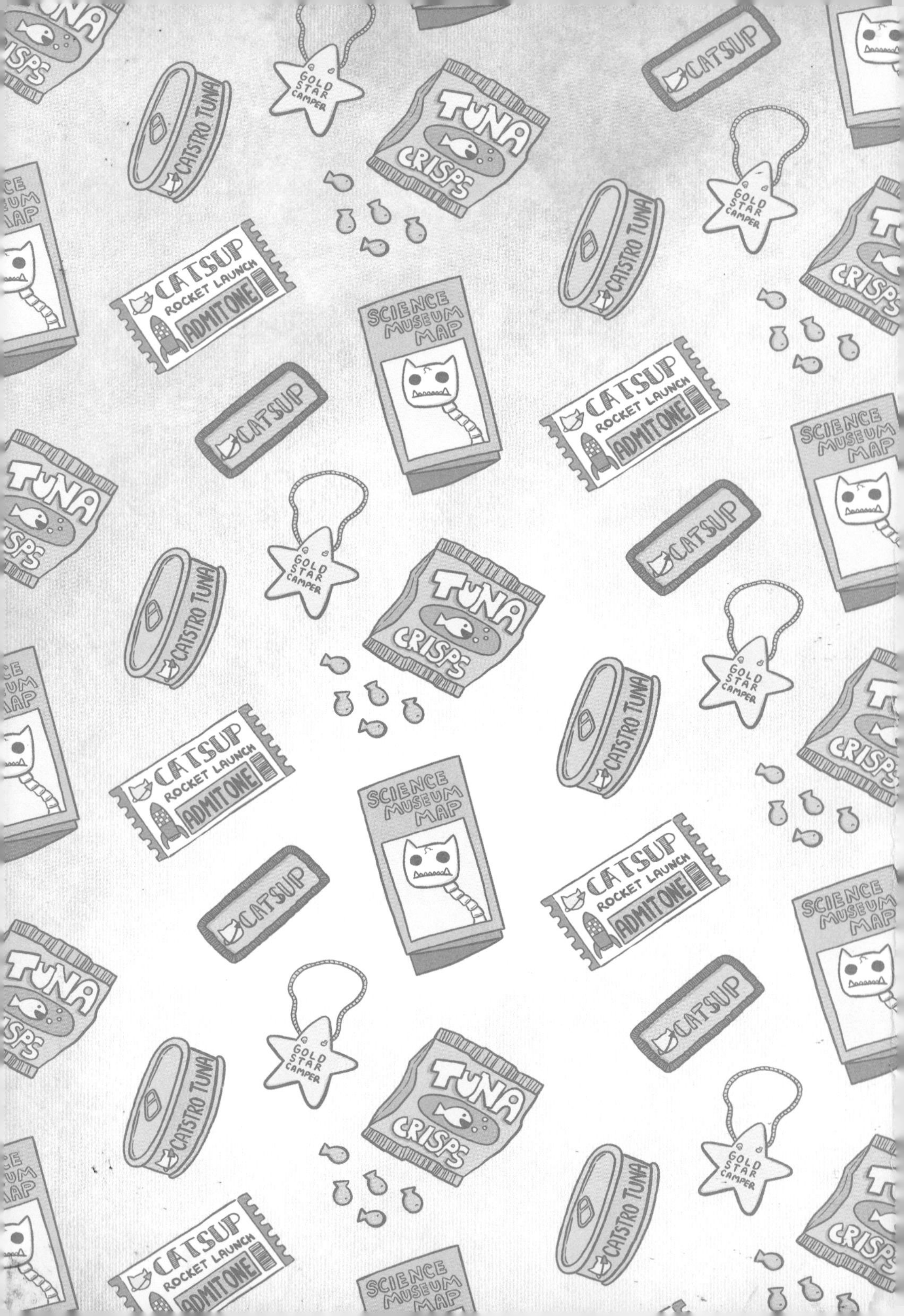
TUNA CRISPS
GOLD STAR CAMPER
CATSTRO TUNA
CATSUP
CATSUP ROCKET LAUNCH ADMIT ONE
SCIENCE MUSEUM MAP